MW01225559

ELECTRIC LITERA- TURE

no.4

COVER
Aaron Johnson
Now We Hunt Hippopotamus
66 x 88 inches
Acrylic on polyester knit mesh
2009
www.aaronjohnsonart.com

INSIDE DRAWINGS
Billy Malone
Ballpoint pen on paper

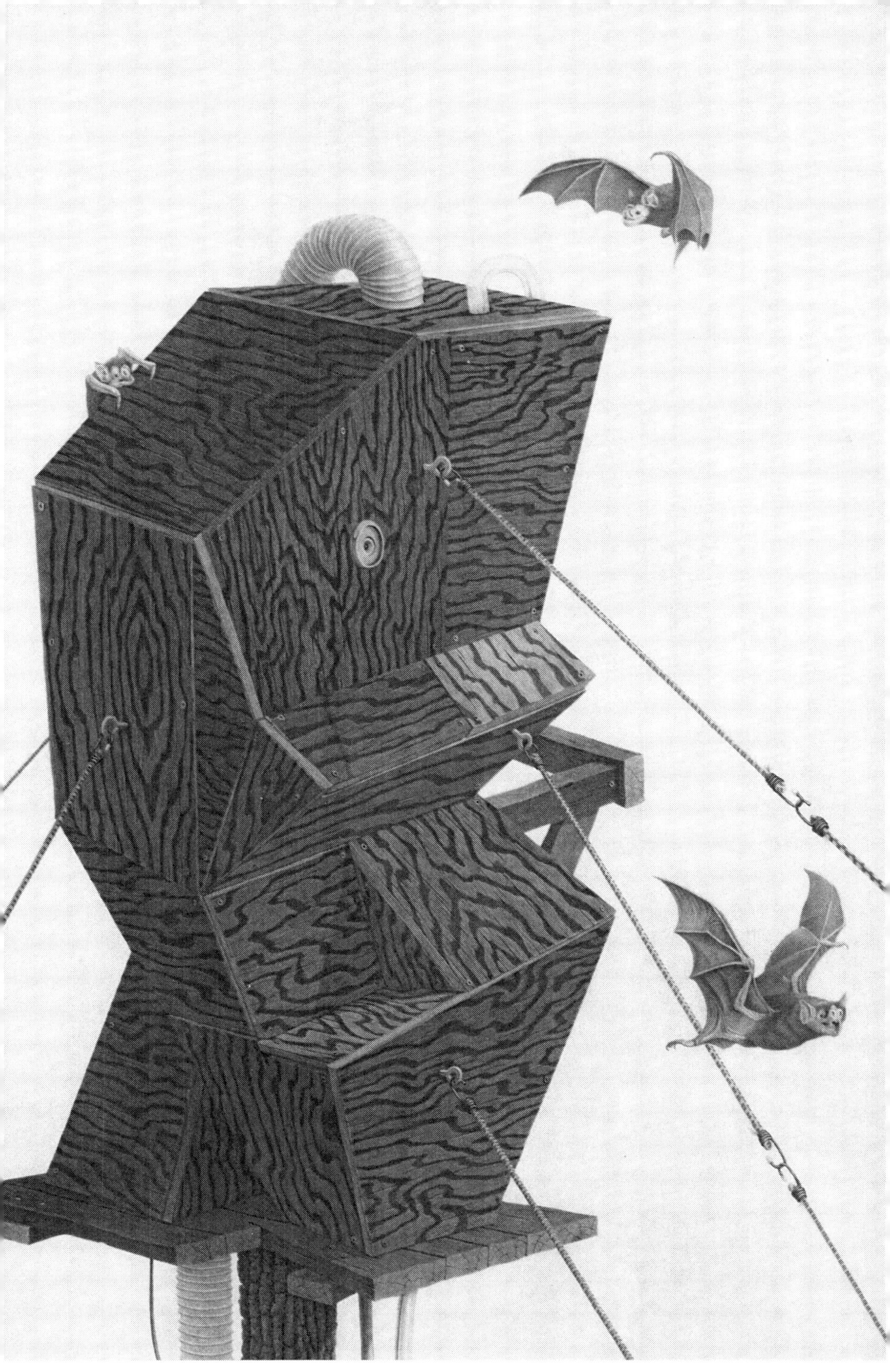

ELECTRIC LITERATURE NO.4

Special Thanks
Jonathan Ashley, Larry Benowich, Melissa Caruso-Scott, Jordan Holberg, Alison Elizabeth Taylor, Brian Lindenbaum, Bruce Lindenbaum, Lydia Millet, Barry Roseman, Alan Roseman, Helen Phillips, Matthew Korahais, David Hirmes, Barbara Epler, Jeremy Mendicino, Kate Bernheimer, Tom Leonard, Mark Subias

"Baba Iaga and the Pelican Child" is forthcoming in *My Mother She Killed Me, My Father He Ate Me: Forty New Fairy Tales*, ed. Kate Bernheimer (Penguin, September 2010)

Electric Literature is published quarterly by Electric Literature, LLC. 325 Gold St. Suite 303, Brooklyn, NY 11201. Email: editors@electricliterature.com.

ISBN 978-0-9824980-6-4

For subscriptions, submission information, or to advertise,
visit our website at **electricliterature.com**

EDITORS' NOTE

Long before we learn to write, we experience the pleasure of being told a story that transports us to a different time, place, and frame of mind. Think about the ineffable magic of the books of your youth; this kind of essential storytelling, from Arabian Nights to Aesop's Fables, is the gateway drug that hooked us on narrative and got us craving the hard stuff. But as literary writers increasingly turned their gazes inward, some of that essential, transportive joy was pruned away from most short stories, or relegated to genre fiction. This issue of Electric Literature recalls that simple pleasure of tale-telling, and the escape and wonder that a fully imagined world can provide.

This issue also marks our first foray into international short fiction, including stories by renowned Spanish author Javier Marías and Mexican author Roberto Ransom (published here in English for the very first time). We're proud to bring these authors to you, and we are planning an issue consisting solely of translated literature later this year.

So what is Electric Literature? Founded by young writers, Electric Literature's mission is to use new media and innovative distribution to keep literature a vital force in popular culture. Our quarterly anthology is streamlined—just five great stories an issue—and available in every viable medium: paperback, Kindle, iPhone, iPad, audiobook, and eBook. We select stories with a strong voice that capture our readers and lead them somewhere exciting, unexpected, and meaningful. We were the first literary magazine to publish on the iPhone and the iPad, the first to launch a YouTube channel, and the first to microserialize a short story on Twitter (@ElectricLit). Visit our website, www.electricliterature.com, and sign up for our email list to stay updated on what's coming next.

Sincerely,
Andy Hunter & Scott Lindenbaum
Editors

electricliterature.com • editors@electricliterature.com

TABLE OF

CONTENTS

BABA IAGA AND THE PELICAN CHILD

By Joy Williams

aba Iaga had a daughter, a pelican child. This did not please her particularly. The pelican child was stunningly strange and beautiful as well as being very very good, which pleased Baba Iaga even less. It was difficult to live as a pelican in the deep dark woods, but the pelican child never seemed to think she belonged to any place other than here with her bony ill-tempered Baba and the cat and the dog. They all lived in a little hut on chicken legs and they were not uncomfortable. Baba Iaga did not care for visitors so when anyone approached, the chicken legs would move in a circle, turning the house so that the visitor could not find the door. This, too, was acceptable to them all.

When Baba Iaga went away—which she did frequently, though she always always returned—she would warn the dog and cat and her beautiful pelican child against allowing strangers into the house. Even if they do not appear as strangers, don't let them in, Baba Iaga said. And she would go off on her strange errands in her iron mortar which she would row through the heavens with a pestle. Often she would return with little fishes which the pelican and the cat relished and the dog did not. The dog had his own cache of food which he consumed judiciously—never too much and never too fast—though he did not hoard it. He was generous and noble to a fault really, though he was shabby and ferocious-looking.

One afternoon when Baba Iaga was away, a tall, somewhat formally attired man approached the house. The chicken legs immediately went into rotation so that the door could not be found (really, the legs looked as if they weren't even awake, but in fact they never slept).

I have heard there is a beautiful bird here, the man shouted out, and I would like to draw her. He waved a sketchbook in the air. I'll make her immortal, he called. The pelican child and the dog and the cat remained sitting quietly in a circle on the floor where they had been playing dominoes. The man remained outside until darkness fell, occasionally calling out to them that he was an artist and very highly regarded. Then he went away. The cat turned on the lamp and they waited for Baba Iaga to return. There were two lamps in the hut, one that illuminated only what they already knew, and another one that Baba Iaga kept locked in a closet that illuminated what they did not know.

Baba Iaga returned and said, I smell something outside. It smells like cruel death. Who has been here? And they described the man and what he had said. If he returns, under no circumstances let him in, Baba Iaga said. The next day she went off once again in her mortar and pestle. On foggy days one could see the faintest trail of her passage through the sky so she brought her broom along to sweep away any trace of herself. Baba Iaga was usually very careful, though sometimes she was not.

The pelican child and the dog and the cat sat in a circle on the floor with their coloring books. The pelican child's favorite color was blue, the cat's black, and the dog pretty much preferred them all, he said. They felt the little house moving and their crayons slid across the floor. Once again the man had returned and the chicken legs had prevented him from finding the door. He shouted up to them as before, proclaiming his devotion to the pelican child's strangeness and beauty and promising to make her immortal. My name is synonymous with beautiful birds, he said, waving his portfolio at the windows.

What is *synonymous*, the dog whispered. He had no idea what it meant and he never would.

Just then the entire forest commenced to rattle, for Baba Iaga had returned and was rushing toward the distinguished gentleman on her bony legs, ready to thrash him with her pestle. Wait, wait, he cried. I only want to create your daughter's portrait. You cannot keep such a splendid creature locked up here. As a mother, you should want her to be appreciated. Others should be allowed to marvel at her. Come, look at the drawings I have made of her avian brothers and sisters.

And Baba Iaga, allowing curiosity to get the better of her and also because she *did* feel somewhat guilty raising her beautiful daughter in the dark woods, agreed to look at the drawings.

They *were* beautiful.

Herons and ibises and egrets and roseate spoonbills and storks, feeding or flying or resting in their nests with their young or gliding above water that sparkled, so great was the gentleman's skill, sunlight pouring through their perfect wings.

Let us retire to your home and lay these pictures on the floor inside so you can study them and they won't be blown about by the wind, he said.

Indeed, a violent wind had come up as though it were trying to tell Baba Iaga something, but she ignored it.

So the chicken legs obediently swung the hut around and Baba Iaga and the gentleman, whose name was John James Audubon, entered.

Well, put out some tea and biscuits for our guest, Baba Iaga snapped at the cat, but the cat said, We have no tea or biscuits. The dog growled but Baba Iaga said to Audubon, Oh, pay no attention to him. This deeply hurt the dog's feelings.

It's quite dim in here, Audubon remarked. Would you have another lamp so that we can see the drawings better? I so want you to approve of them so you will allow me to draw your beautiful daughter.

I do have another lamp, Baba Iaga said gladly.

And please, grandmother, he said, could you be so kind as to lock the dog and cat away? The dog does frighten me a bit and I'm allergic to cats.

Baba Iaga put the dog and the cat in the closet and followed them in, looking for the other lamp. Oh, wouldn't you know, she muttered, I put it on the highest, most difficult-to-reach shelf. Audubon slammed the door shut and bolted it. Baba Iaga and the dog and the cat were so stunned that for a moment they were completely speechless. Then they heard their beautiful pelican child say, Oh, please sir, do not take me from this bright world! And then a sharp crack as though from a pistol, then terrible sounds of pain and surprise, and then nothing. The dog began to howl and the cat to hiss. Baba Iaga beat on the door with her bony hands and feet which were sharp as a horse's hooves, but the door was old and strong, the wood practically petrified, and they could not break through it. But the dog flung himself against the door again and again and worried a sliver loose with his teeth and claws, and then another sliver. He did not know how long he tore at the door. He had no conception of time. It seemed only yesterday he was a puppy, hanging onto Baba Iaga's sock as she limped across the room, or pouncing at moths, or grinning with joy when he was allowed (before he got too big) to accompany Baba Iaga on her flights across the sky. It seemed only yesterday when his fur was soft and black, his paws so pink and tender, his teeth so white, or it seemed as though it could be tomorrow.

Finally, he had made a hole in the door just large enough for him to crawl through. What met his eyes was a scene so horrific he could not understand it. He began to tremble and howl. The beautiful pelican child was pierced through with cruel rods and was arranged in a position of life, her great wings extended, her elegant neck arched. But her life had been taken away, and her eyes were fathomless and dark. A *specimen*, the cat screamed behind him. He has made of our sister a specimen! And then he felt the tears of Baba Iaga striking him like hail.

He left. Outside, he ran and ran through the forest. He could see the man running too, clutching his wretched papers and pens. Often the dog stumbled and twice he fell, for his hips had been bad for some time and his poor old heart now pounded with sorrow. At last he gave up the pursuit, for the evil one had far outdistanced him. After he rested and caught his breath, he smelled the dreadful scent of cruel death. Audubon's abandoned campsite was nearby and a fire of green branches still smoldered. Many trees had been cut down, and on their stumps were colorful woodland birds, thrushes and larks and woodpeckers and tiny iridescent and colorfully patterned ones whose names the dog did not know. Long nails thrust through their small bodies kept them erect, and thread and wire held their heads and kept their wings aloft. Even more horrifying was the sight of birds dismembered, their pinions and claws severed for study. Whimpering, the dog fled and after he had gone a short distance or a long distance, after a long time or a short time, he came to the little hut on chicken legs. The legs were weeping and Baba Iaga and the cat were weeping. Baba Iaga had enfolded her daughter in her arms, and her tears fell without ceasing on the pelican child's brown breast.

In the morning, the cat said, We must do something.

I will go out again and find him and tear him to pieces, the dog said wearily.

I don't give a rat's ass about Audubon, the cat said. We must bring our beautiful pelican sister back.

Perhaps we should call for Prince Ivan, the dog suggested.

Useless, Baba Iaga said. He has his princess and his castle. He never calls, he never writes, he is of no use to us.

We will put the beautiful pelican child in the oven, the cat announced.

I couldn't bear to put my daughter in the cold cold oven, Baba Iaga said.

Who said anything about cold? the cat said. We will preheat it to oh say, two hundred fifty degrees and we will put her in for only half an hour.

Half an hour? the dog said.

That stove hasn't been used in years, Baba Iaga said.

But they did what the cat suggested, for what else could they do?

Carefully, they lay the pelican child in the oven, which was no longer cold, but not too warm either. Oh, her beautiful face, Baba Iaga cried, her beautiful bill, take care with her bill.

Then they waited.

Has it been half an hour yet? the dog asked.

Not yet, the cat said.

At last the cat announced that it had been half an hour. Baba Iaga opened the oven and the pelican child, as beautiful as she had ever been, tumbled out and tottered into their happy arms, alive.

After this, Baba Iaga continued to fly through the skies in her mortar, navigating with her pestle. But instead of a broom, she carried the lamp that illuminated the things people did not know or were reluctant or refused to understand. And she would lower the lamp over a person and they would see how extraordinary were the birds and beasts of the world, and that they should be valued for their bright and beautiful and mysterious selves and not willfully harmed, for they were more precious than castles or the golden rocks dug out from the earth.

But she could reach only a few people each day with the lamp.

Once, seven experienced its light, but usually it was far less. It would take thousands of years, tens of thousands of years perhaps, to reach all human beings with the light.

Baba Iaga came home one evening—so tired—and she gathered her little family around her, the pelican child and the dog and the cat and said, My dear ones, I still have magic and power unrealized. Do you wish to become human beings? For some think you are under a hellish spell. Do you want to become human? The cat and the dog spoke. The pelican child had not spoken since the day of her return.

No, the dog and the cat said.

THE RESIGNATION LETTER OF SEÑOR DE SANTIESTEBAN

By Javier Marías

•

For Juan Benet, fifteen years late

hether it was one of those bizarre occurrences to which Chance never quite manages to accustom us, however often they may arise; or whether Destiny, in a show of prudence, temporarily suspended judgment on the qualities and attributes of the new teacher and delayed intervening, in case such an intervention should later turn out to be a mistake; the fact of the matter is that young Mr. Lilburn did not discover the truth in the strange warnings issued to him by his superior, Mr. Bayo, and other colleagues only a few days after he had joined the Institute, until he was well into the first term and sufficient time had elapsed for him to forget, or at least to postpone thinking about, the possible significance of the warnings. Mr. Lilburn, in any case, belonged to that class of person who, sooner or later, in the course of a hitherto untroubled life, finds his career in ruins and his unshakable beliefs overturned, refuted, and even held up to ridicule by just such an event as concerns us here. It would, therefore, have made little difference if he had never been asked to stay behind to lock up the building.

Lilburn, who was just thirty-one, had eagerly accepted the post offered him by Mr. Bayo, the director of the British Institute in Madrid. Indeed, he had experienced a sense of relief and the muted joy felt in such situations by men who—while they would never dare even to dream of rising to heights they had already accepted would never be theirs—nevertheless expect some small improvement in their position as the most natural thing in the world. And although his work at the Institute did not, in itself, constitute any economic or social improvement with respect to his previous position, young Mr. Lilburn was very conscious that, while spending nine months abroad was almost an invitation for people in his native city to forget all about him, and implied the loss—perhaps not, he imagined, irrevocable—of his comfortable but mediocre post at the North London Polytechnic, it also brought the possibility of coming into contact with people higher up the administrative ladder and, more importantly, with prestigious members of the diplomatic corps. Having dealings, for example (why not?), with an ambassador could prove most useful to him, however sporadic and superficial those dealings might be. And so, around the middle of September, with the indifference of any only moderately ambitious man, he made his preparations, recommending a far less knowledgeable replacement for the post he was vacating at the Polytechnic, and arriving in Madrid, determined to work hard if necessary to earn the esteem and trust of his superiors—with an eye to any future advantages this might bring him—and resolved not to allow himself to be seduced by the flexibility of the Spanish working day.

Young Lilburn soon established an orderly life for himself in that foreign land and, after a few initial days of vacillation and relative bewilderment—days he was obliged to spend in the house of old Mr. Bayo and his wife while he waited for the previous tenants to vacate the small furnished attic apartment reserved for him in Calle de Orellana (the rent exceeded Lilburn's budget, but it wasn't really expensive if one took into account its central location and proximity to the Institute)—he set himself a meticulous daily routine, which he managed to strictly maintain until the month of March. He got up at seven on the dot and, after breakfasting at home and briefly going over what he planned to say in each of his morning classes, set off to the Institute to teach. During break-time, he would share with Mr. Bayo and Miss Ferris his dismay at the Spanish students' appalling lack of discipline and then, over lunch, would make the same remarks to Mr. Turol and Mr. White. Over dessert, he would review the afternoon's lessons at a rather slower pace than he had in the morning, and, once they were over, would spend from six to half past seven in the Institute's library, consulting a few books and preparing his classes for the next day. He would then walk to the elegant house of the widowed Señora Giménez-Klein in Calle Fortuny to give an hour's private tutoring to her eight-year-old granddaughter (his protector, Mr. Bayo, had found him this simple, well-remunerated work), and then return to his apartment in Calle Orellana at about half past nine or shortly thereafter, in time to hear the radio news: although at first Lilburn understood almost nothing, he was convinced that this was the best way to learn correct Spanish pronunciation. He then ate a light supper, read a couple of chapters of his Spanish grammar book, hurriedly memorized vast lists of verbs and nouns, and went to bed punctually at half past eleven.

Lilburn's life was methodical and ordered, and his feet probably took no more than two thousand steps each day. His weekends, however—with the exception of the occasional Saturday when he attended suppers or receptions for visitors from British universities (and, on just one occasion, a cocktail party at the embassy)—were a mystery to his colleagues and superiors, who supposed, based on the not-very-revealing circumstance that he never answered the phone on those days, that he must go on short trips to nearby towns. It would seem, however, that at least until January or February, young Lilburn spent Saturdays and Sundays closeted in his apartment struggling with the whims and caprices of Spanish conjugations. And one could only assume that he spent his Christmas vacation in the same way.

Derek Lilburn was a man of little imagination, ordinary tastes, and an insignficant past. The only son of mediocre, second-tier actors who had achieved a certain degree of popularity (if not prestige) during the early part of the Second World War with an Elizabethan and Jacobean repertoire that included Massinger, Beaumont & Fletcher, and Heywood the Younger, but scrupulously avoided authors of greater stature like Marlowe, Webster, or, indeed, Shakespeare, Lilburn had nonetheless failed to inherit what used to be called "a vocation for the stage"; although one might well question whether his progenitors had ever harbored such a vocation themselves. When the war was over and the various divas, hungry for applause, hurried back to the theater, the Lilburns, apparently without regret, left the capital and the profession. They settled in Swansea and opened a grocery store. All that remained of those eventful times were a few posters advertising *Philaster* and *The Revenger's Tragedy.* Neither books nor erudition were accoutrements of young Lilburn's childhood, and you can be quite sure that he did not even benefit from the one vestige that unwittingly remained of his parents' years spent treading the boards: an emphatic, smug, or affected way of speaking even in banal, domestic conversation.

The death of his father, which occurred when young Derek was just eighteen, meant that he could take personal charge of the business, and the death of his mother a few months later served as a good excuse to sell the establishment, move to London, and pay for his own higher education. Once he had gained his degree, with the illusory brilliance of the diligent student, he worked as a teacher in state schools for a few years—without being assailed by any vocational doubts—until 1969, when, thanks to a superficial and entirely self-interested friendship with a teacher at the Polytechnic, he was appointed to the very post he had now rejected in favor of this brief stay abroad—a period which he somehow sensed would be a transitional one.

• • •

It is well-known to all those familiar with the Institute, whether as teachers, students, or merely as regular visitors to the library, that its doors close at nine o'clock sharp (half an hour after the last evening classes end). The person charged with closing up is the porter, whose duties often depart from those implied by his title and more closely resemble those of a librarian or beadle. This man must keep an eye on the entrances and exits of anyone not employed by the Institute; attend to any orders, errands, or demands issued by teachers; clean the blackboards, which, for reasons of carelessness or forgetfulness, have been left covered in numbers, illustrious names, and notable dates; ensure that no one takes a book from the library without its loan having been duly recorded; and, finally—leaving aside a few lesser tasks—make quite certain that, at five minutes to nine, the building is empty and, if it is, lock the doors until the following morning.

Fabián Jaunedes, the man occupying the busy post of porter when young Derek Lilburn arrived in Madrid, had, for twenty-four years, been carrying out his duties with the perfection of one who has almost created his own job. And so when, in early March, he was admitted to the hospital with some haste and urgency for a cataract operation and thus forced to abandon his duties for at least as long as it would take him to recuperate (a recuperation that would necessarily be incomplete or partial and which would, at any rate, take far longer than those running the Institute might desire), the internal life of the school suffered far worse disruption than one would have thought. The Director and Mr. Bayo immediately rejected the idea of taking on a replacement, for, on the one hand, at such short notice it would be hard to find someone with good references prepared to commit himself for what little remained of the semester, only to find himself possibly replaced (they doubted the old porter would make such a speedy recovery, but it seemed to them that filling the vacant position for more than five months was tantamount to getting rid of Fabián for good, which would be a gross act of disloyalty to someone who had himself been so loyal and given such good service for so many years). On the other hand, they soon revealed that ability or obscure need to turn a minor sacrifice or compromise into something truly epic—an ability or need so prevalent among the unimaginative and among people of a certain age—when they decided that, in view of this unexpected setback (which they would have described, rather, as an adversity), it would not be unreasonable to call for a minor sacrifice on the part of each of the teachers, who could easily share the absent porter's various duties and demonstrate *en passant* their selfless devotion to the Institute. The librarian was left in charge of keeping an eye on any strangers who went in and out of the main door, which she could easily see from her usual position; Miss Ferris was to keep the flyers and announcements on the bulletin boards in the entrance hall up-to-date, without allowing too many to accumulate; every few hours, Mr. Turol was to inspect the state of the toilets and the boiler; those teachers who finished their classes at half past eight were urged to appoint one of their students to clean the blackboard before leaving; and, lastly, among the members of staff who had not been assigned any specific task, an equitable rota was put in place: someone must remain in the building until nine at night to check that all was in order and to lock the doors. Although this represented a disturbance to Lilburn's rigid routine, he had no alternative but to miss his appointment with Señora Giménez-Klein's granddaughter one evening a week and to collaborate with his superiors and colleagues on the smooth running of the Institute by staying in the library until nine o'clock every Friday from March onwards.

It was on the first Friday when he was called upon to perform this new duty that Mr. Bayo revived in his memory—with the same nonchalance that had made an astonished Lilburn wonder if this earnest man with his irreproachable manners was really capable of such an outrageous assertion—that initial warning which, when he'd first arrived, had produced in him a certain feeling of unease.

"Now, tonight," Mr. Bayo said to him during break-time, "as I explained to you once before, don't worry about the ghost. I believe I mentioned it briefly when you joined us, but I thought I'd better remind you in case you'd forgotten, since you might be startled by the noises Señor de Santiesteban makes. At a quarter to nine, you'll hear a door burst open, then seven footsteps in one direction and, after a pause, eight footsteps back. The door that opened will then close, more quietly this time. There's no need to be frightened or to take any notice of it. This is something that has been happening since who knows when, certainly for as long as the Institute has had its headquarters in this building. It has nothing whatsoever to do with us, and as you can imagine, we're more than used to it—as, of course, is poor Fabián, who's usually the only person to hear it.

"Just one thing: given that you will have the keys over the weekend and will, therefore, be the first to arrive on Monday morning to open up, please don't forget to remove his letter of resignation from the bulletin board opposite my office. Be sure to do this as soon as you come in. Although everyone knows of Señor de Santiesteban's existence (we don't hide it from anyone, I can assure you, and no one is troubled or upset by his presence, which is, besides, most discreet), we nevertheless try not to let it intrude too much on the lives of the students, who, being children, are more sensitive than we are to such inexplicable events. So please do remember to remove the letter. And, of course, simply throw it in the nearest garbage can. Imagine what it would be like if we kept them! By now we'd have a whole roomful of them. When I think about it, it all seems utterly ridiculous! Night after night, at the same hour, the same identical letter, with not a single word or syllable different. That, you'll agree, is what you'd call perseverance."

Young Lilburn responded only with a nod.

• • •

But as night fell, and he was sitting in the library grading papers until it was time to lock up the building and go home, he heard a door being flung open so violently that it rattled the glass panes; then a few firm, resolute—not to say mutinous—steps followed by a brief silence that lasted only seconds; then more steps, returning, calmer this time; and, finally, the same door (one presumes) gently closing. Lilburn looked at the clock hanging on the wall and saw that it was eight forty-six. Feeling more irritated than surprised or alarmed, he got up and left the library. In the corridor, he stopped and listened, expecting to hear new noises, but there was nothing. Then he scoured the building in search of some laggardly student or joker to whom he would try to demonstrate the pointlessness of his prank, but he found no one.

Nine o'clock struck, and he decided to leave and think no more about the matter; however, just as he was about to leave, he remembered another of Mr. Bayo's instructions, possibly the one that had most stuck in his mind: he went up to the second floor to inspect the bulletin board in the corridor immediately opposite his superior's office. All he saw there, affixed with four thumb tacks, was an already much-read leaflet announcing a series of talks on George Darley and other minor romantic poets, due to be given by a visiting lecturer from Brasenose College beginning in April. But there was absolutely nothing remotely resembling a letter of resignation. Feeling calmer and also rather pleased, he set off towards Calle de Orellana and thought no more about the episode until Monday, around mid-morning, when Miss Ferris came up to him after one of his classes and informed him that Mr. Bayo wished to see him in his office.

"Mr. Lilburn," said the old history teacher when he went in, "don't you remember my urging you, before you did anything else this morning, to remove Señor de Santiesteban's resignation letter from the bulletin board outside?"

"Yes, sir, I remember perfectly. But on Friday night, after I'd heard the footsteps you warned me about, I went up to do exactly that, but found no letter on the board. Should I have looked again this morning?"

Mr. Bayo struck his forehead like someone who has suddenly understood something and replied:

"Of course, it's my fault for not having warned you. Yes, Mr. Lilburn, you need *only* look at the bulletin board in the morning. Not that it matters, this is hardly the first time it's happened. But next Friday, remember: the letters only appear at dawn, even though one would imagine that Señor de Santiesteban would pin them to the notice board at a quarter to nine. Yes, I know it's inexplicable, but then so is the very presence of the gentleman himself, is it not? Well, that was all I wanted to say, Mr. Lilburn, but don't worry, the children will have calmed down by this afternoon."

"The children?"

"Yes, it was the juniors who brought it to my notice that the letters were still there. I heard them talking excitedly in the corridor, went out to see what was going on, and found the boys all very worked up, handing round the three sheets of paper."

Lilburn made an exasperated gesture and said:

"I don't understand a word, Mr. Bayo. I really would be most grateful if you could give me a detailed and coherent account of the facts. What is all this about three letters, for example? What is the story behind this ghost, if he really exists? You keep talking about letters of resignation, but I still don't know what the devil it is that this Señor de Santiesteban fellow resigns from each night. I'm totally bewildered and don't know what to think."

Mr. Bayo gave a faint, melancholy smile and said:

"Nor do I, Mr. Lilburn, and believe me, after all my years here, I, too, would like to know the details of Señor de Santiesteban's undoubtedly sad story. But we know absolutely nothing about him. His name tells us nothing, nor does it appear in any yearbooks, dictionaries, or encyclopedias of any kind: he wasn't famous, or rather, he did nothing in his life worthy of mention. Perhaps he was in some way linked to the former owner of the building, the man who had it built around 1930—I can't remember the exact date now—he was an immensely wealthy man, interested in the arts and in politics; he was a kind of patron of left-wing intellectuals during the time of the Second Republic, and he died bankrupt. But we don't know for sure, nor, indeed, do we have any concrete information that allows us to assume any relationship. Then again, it could be that his close association with the building stems from his acquaintance, friendship, or professional involvement with the architect, who was an equally interesting character: his ideas were quite advanced for the time, but he committed suicide, jumping overboard during an Atlantic crossing when he was still relatively young. Again, there's no way of finding out. All of this is mere supposition, Mr. Lilburn, mere hypothesizing that I don't even dare to formulate in its entirety because there are so few facts."

"It's all very strange, very curious," remarked Lilburn.

"It certainly is," said Mr. Bayo. "And I have to say that a long time ago, when I was only a little older than you are now and had just started work at the Institute, Señor de Santiesteban's mysterious footsteps aroused my curiosity and even robbed me of my sleep for some months; I wouldn't be exaggerating if I said that they came close to becoming an obsession. I neglected my work and devoted myself to making inquiries. I visited the relatives of the former owner and of the architect and asked them about a possible friendship between either of those two men and one Leandro P. de Santiesteban, but they had never heard of him. I consulted the telephone book in search of someone called Pérez de Santiesteban, for example (because I still don't know what the P stands for: perhaps the first part of a double-barreled last name, perhaps simply Pedro, Patricio, Plácido, I don't know), but I found none; in my overwhelming desire to know the ghost's story, I went to the registry office in the hope that I might find a birth certificate that would at least give me a trail to follow, even if it was a false one: a similar last name so that I could at least focus my investigations on something, but I got no positive results, only problems with various bureaucrats who took me for a madman, and with the police, because my behavior, in those alarmist times, seemed very suspicious indeed. Finally, I went to visit all the Santiestebans in the city, and there are quite a few. But those I spoke with told me there had never been anyone called Leandro in their family, while others refused to even talk to me. In short, it was all in vain, and I finally had to abandon my search, with the disagreeable feeling of having wasted my time and made a complete fool of myself. Now, like the other people who work at the Institute, I simply accept the ghost's undeniable existence and pay him not the slightest heed, because I know there's no point; taking any interest at all brings only trouble and discontent. And so I'm very sorry, Mr. Lilburn, but I can't answer your questions. I would only advise you to ignore Señor de Santiesteban like everyone else. Don't worry, he's not dangerous; he simply leaves a resignation letter each night and we remove it the following day."

"That's precisely what I was going to ask you. Doesn't the resignation letter explain something? What is he resigning from? And why, as you said earlier, were there three letters today?"

Mr. Bayo bent towards the wastepaper basket beside him, removed a few crumpled sheets of paper and held them out to Lilburn, saying:

"There were three of them today for the simple reason that today is Monday and, as usual, there was no one in the building over the weekend to take down the letters from Friday, Saturday, and Sunday. You should have removed them from the bulletin board first thing this morning, but as I said, that was my fault, not yours. Here."

Lilburn took the sheets of very ordinary paper and read them carefully. They had been written with a fountain pen, and the words were the same on all three, without the slightest variation:

> *Dear Friend,*
> *In view of the regrettable events of recent days, the nature of which run counter not only to my habits, but to my principles, I have no alternative, even though I am well aware of the grave difficulties my decision will cause you, of resigning forthwith from my post. And may I say, too, that I strenuously disapprove of and condemn your attitude to the aforementioned events.*
>
> *Leandro P. de Santiesteban*

"As you see," said Mr. Bayo, "the letter reveals nothing; in fact, it only serves to make the whole business even more baffling, given that this building was a private residence and not an office—that is, not a place occupied by people with posts from which they could resign. We have to be satisfied with merely contemplating the enigma without trying to decipher it."

• • •

The months of March and April came and went, and each Friday, young Lilburn, sitting in the library, would listen to Señor de Santiesteban's unvarying footsteps on the floor above. He tried to follow Mr. Bayo's advice and ignore those mysterious steps, but sometimes, unexpectedly, he would find himself pondering the ghost's personality and history, or mechanically counting the number of steps in each direction. In this respect, he had discovered that, as his superior had told him on one occasion, Señor de Santiesteban always took seven steps in one direction and then, after a pause, eight steps back, after which he closed the door. It was during the Easter vacation, which he spent in Toledo, that a possible explanation for this occurred to him. He was extremely excited by this tiny discovery—which was, in fact, no more than mere conjecture whose truth he would be unable to verify—and he longed for the moment when he could return to Madrid and tell Mr. Bayo.

On the first day back after the holidays, instead of staying in the playground during break, exchanging complaints with Miss Ferris and Mr. Bayo about the unsatisfactory behavior of their students, young Lilburn asked Mr. Bayo if they could go somewhere private to talk in peace and, once they were ensconced in the old history teacher's office, Lilburn lay his discovery before him.

"In my opinion," he said, slightly nervous, "the reason Señor de Santiesteban takes first seven steps and then eight is this: outraged by the events to which he refers in his letter and which prevent him, a man of principle, from remaining in his post, he storms out of the room in which he is sitting and takes seven steps—or should I say strides—over to the bulletin board. He leaves his letter there, and, feeling calmer now that he has done his duty, now that he's broken with the friend who has so disappointed him, and now that his conscience is clear, he returns to his room, taking eight steps instead of seven because he is now less angry or agitated, and may even be feeling rather pleased with himself. The proof of this, Mr. Bayo, is the fact that he then closes the door slowly, without the anger evident in the violence with which he flung it open."

"You put the case very well, Mr. Lilburn," replied Mr. Bayo with barely-perceptible irony. "And I think you're right. I myself reached the same conclusion many years ago when I, too, took an interest in the matter. But it got me nowhere imagining that the different number of steps taken in each direction was due to a slight change in Señor de Santiesteban's mood. Here I am, as ignorant as I was on my first day. Listen: the enigma of the Institute's ghost is just that, an enigma. There is no way it can be deciphered."

Mr. Lilburn thought for a moment, somewhat disappointed by Mr. Bayo's cool response. After a few seconds, however, he looked up and asked:

"Wouldn't it be possible to speak to him?"

"Speak to whom? To Señor de Santiesteban? No. Let me explain: on Friday night at a quarter to nine, you hear the door of this office being flung open, as you would on any other evening of the week if you happened to be in the Institute; then you hear footsteps and the door closing again. That's right, isn't it?"

"It is."

"And where are you usually sitting when this happens?"

"In the library."

"Well, if, instead of sitting in the library, you were in this office or, indeed, outside in the corridor, you would hear exactly the same thing, but you would also see that the door does not open. You *hear* it opening and closing, but you can *see* that it neither opens nor closes; it remains in its place, motionless: the glass panes don't even rattle when you hear the door being flung open initially."

"I see. And are you absolutely sure that it's this door and not another door that the ghost opens?"

"Yes. It's definitely that glass-paned door behind you. Believe me, I've checked. When I was sure that this was the case, I spent a few nights here, watching it. As you said before, Señor de Santiesteban storms out of this office, goes over to the bulletin board, pins up his letter of resignation, and comes back. The letter, however, doesn't appear at once, but at some point during the night or in the early hours—precisely when, I don't know. The only two occasions on which I managed to remain awake, without once nodding off and thus giving Señor de Santiesteban a chance to pin up his letter, I heard the usual footsteps, but the letter never appeared. That must mean that he saw that I was awake, which is why the letter didn't appear.

"But he refuses to speak or perhaps cannot speak. After those two nights, when I realized that I, in turn, was being watched by him (or, rather, although I couldn't see him, he was watching my every move), I addressed him on several occasions and in diverse tones of voice: one day, I greeted him respectfully, the next, mellifluously, the day after that, angrily. I even went so far as to insult him, just to see if he would react.

But he never responded; nothing worked, and so I did the best thing I could have done: I abandoned my stupid, naïve vigils and came to think of Don Leandro P. de Santiesteban just as everyone else here does, as 'the Institute's remarkable ghost.'"

Young Lilburn again thought for a few moments and then said with real concern:

"But, Mr. Bayo... if everything you have told me is true, then Señor de Santiesteban must inhabit this office, and might well be listening to us now, isn't that so?"

"Possibly, Mr. Lilburn," responded Mr. Bayo, "possibly."

• • •

From that day forth, young Lilburn did not speak to Mr. Bayo or to anyone else about the Institute's ghost. The old teacher assumed, with some relief, that Lilburn had concluded that giving any further thought to the matter was a waste of time and had decided to follow his advice, born of long experience. This was not, however, the case. Young Lilburn, behind his superior's back, and in a rather improvised fashion, had decided to find out for himself what drove Señor de Santiesteban to resign from his post every night. Since he was left in charge of the keys over the weekend and could therefore come and go as he pleased, he had started spending Friday, Saturday, and Sunday nights on the sofa in the second-floor corridor, where, even lying down, he had a clear view of the entire, albeit rather limited, stage occupied by the invisible ghost's nocturnal walks: the door of Mr. Bayo's office, the bulletin board opposite, and, of course, the space between.

There were three reasons, or rather, feelings, that drove him to carry out his investigations in secret: suspicion, the lure of the clandestine, and the sheer challenge of the thing. He made good use of Mr. Bayo's generous account of events and of the lessons to be learned from his failure, but at the same time, he felt that if he was to fulfill his desire to solve the mystery, he had to experience for himself at least some of the setbacks that this same ambition had inflicted on his superior in the past. He also found in those long periods of waiting the pleasure one always gets from experiencing anything that is forbidden or unknown to the rest of humanity. And finally, he savored in advance the moment when his endeavors would be crowned with victory, which consisted not only in securing and forever possessing the longed-for truth, but also in enjoying the inner satisfaction—from which vanity definitely derives the most pleasure—implicit in any triumph over a more important and more knowledgeable opponent.

And in the months that followed, the last of the school year, young Lilburn suffered the same setbacks as the old history teacher had in his youth. He tried without success to speak to Señor de Santiesteban; he waited patiently, again and again, for the letter to appear on the bulletin board, but sooner or later, being obliged as he was to remain for hours with his eyes fixed on one point, sleep almost always overcame him; and on the two or three occasions when he did manage to keep his eyes open until the next morning, the letter did not appear.

Time passed rapidly, and he was left with ever fewer opportunities to attain his objective. Dissatisfied with the abominable behavior of his Spanish students and with his work, which had brought him few chances to improve his position in the short term, he had resolved not to renew his contract for another year and to return to his job at the Polytechnic in London as soon as the term was over. However, as the end-of-school activities drew nearer, Lilburn came to regret more and more having taken that stance. Now that he had his ticket home, he could not go back on his decision, and he repeatedly berated himself for his precipitate behavior when, in a sudden, irrational rush of confidence, he had thought that success was only a matter of weeks away. He could see the day approaching when he would have to leave, doubtless never to return, and he ceaselessly cursed his excessive optimism and the cold indifference of Señor de Santiesteban, who treated him as haughtily as he had Mr. Bayo, and—even more woundingly—other mere mortals as well. In his madness, listening for the nth time to the sound of the footsteps on the wooden floor, he would try to grab the ghost or shout at him, calling him a vain, cowardly, heartless fraud—in short, heaping him with insults.

However, on just such an occasion, he came up with a possible remedy for his despair, a solution to his ignorance. A moment before, he had been through one of those stormy episodes provoked by the ghost's disdain for him, and, feeling desolate and in the grip of the hysterical rage induced by situations of prolonged impotence, he had lain face down on the sofa in the corridor. It was eight forty-seven. Suddenly, in the midst of his anguish, he seemed to hear the door to Mr. Bayo's office flung open and Señor de Santiesteban again taking his invariable fifteen steps before once more closing the door, as he always did. Surprised, he sat up and smoothed his dishevelled hair. He looked at the door and then at the bulletin board. And that was when he realized that he hadn't actually heard anything the second time, but that, like a piece of music on a record one has played and re-played throughout the day, the footsteps, their rhythm and intensity, had lodged in his brain and were being repeated inside him, unwittingly, involuntarily, like an obsessive, particularly complicated passage that one remembers perfectly and yet cannot reproduce. He knew them by heart, and although it was, of course, impossible to imitate them with his voice, he could with his own feet. Buoyed up by new hope and enthusiasm, he left the building. And on that Saturday in June, for the first time in many weekends, he slept in his apartment in Calle de Orellana.

He suddenly felt like an actor who has spent several months performing in the same play with considerable success and who, knowing that the audience will reward his performance with a warm round of applause, is in no hurry to appear onstage to play his part, but rather, allows himself the luxury of lingering in the wings and making his entrance a few seconds late so as to create a sense of expectation among the audience and slight alarm among his fellow actors. Lilburn, then, felt so confident of his success that instead of putting his plan into action straight away, he devoted himself—although not without having to struggle against his own pressing feelings of uncertainty—to revelling in the good fortune that Destiny, he sensed, was about to bestow on him. He spent only one more typical night at the Institute, on the eve of his departure and his encounter with Señor de Santiesteban. Indeed, he decided to wait until all the classes and exams were over before carrying out his experiment, and he felt that his last full day would be the most appropriate date to choose, for the following reason: if anything out of the ordinary happened to him, no one would miss him or, in consequence, make any awkward or compromising investigations, given that everyone, including Mr. Bayo, would imagine that he was in London and so would find nothing odd about his absence.

And although that night, between eight and half past nine, the students would be putting on their traditional end-of-term theatrical production, which would mean that on that particular Saturday he would be far from alone in the building, he felt that this would, in fact, only work in his favor (on the one hand, no one would trouble him, because at a quarter to nine, parents, teachers, students, and cleaning ladies would all be in the auditorium, and, on the other hand, if anyone did surprise him in the act, his presence at that hour in the Institute would be more than justified): all these factors only increased his determination. Just in case, though, he left nothing to chance: he found it easy enough to persuade Mr. Bayo to lend him his office key and to have a copy made; he synchronized his watch with the Institute clock and checked that neither was running slow or fast; and as I mentioned before, he spent the whole of the previous night rehearsing, until he had an absolutely perfect imitation down.

The day came. Lilburn made his appearance shortly before eight o'clock and was greatly praised for having turned up at the Institute to see the performance even though he was due to fly to London that very night at half past eleven. He took advantage of this circumstance to warn that, precisely because he had a plane to catch, he would, most regrettably, have to leave halfway through the production, adding that he was nevertheless very glad to be able to see at least a good part of it before leaving. Just as the performance was about to begin, he said goodbye to his colleagues and to Mr. Bayo, to whom he said, "You'll be hearing from me."

That year, the students were putting on a shortened version of *Julius Caesar*. Both the acting and the diction were appalling, but Lilburn barely noticed, immersed as he was in his own thoughts. And at twenty-two minutes to nine, at the beginning of the third act, he stood up, and, trying not to make too much noise, left the auditorium and walked up to the second floor. He unlocked Mr. Bayo's office door and went in.

There he waited for a few more minutes and then, when it was exactly eight forty-five by his watch, and he could hear in the distance the voice of a boy saying, "I know not, gentlemen, what you intend, who else must be let blood, who else is rank," young Derek Lilburn flung open the door, making the glass panes rattle, took seven determined steps over to the notice board, pinned up a sheet of ordinary paper with one thumb tack, took another eight steps in the opposite direction, went back into the office, and closed the door gently behind him.

• • •

Over the summer, old Fabián Jaunedes lost his sight completely, and Mr. Bayo and the director of the Institute had no option but to hire a new porter. When the new incumbent arrived on September 1st to take up his post, Mr. Bayo told him about Señor de Santiesteban and about the letter of resignation. As he usually did—feeling fearful, moreover, on this occasion, that the new arrival might take fright and decide not to accept the post—he tried to play it down and provide as few details as possible. The new porter, who, as well as having impeccable references, had excellent manners and knew his place, merely nodded respectfully and assured Mr. Bayo that he would remember to remove the letter from the bulletin-board each morning. The old history teacher breathed a sigh of relief and told himself that acquiring the services of such a man had been a real coup. However, imagine his surprise the next morning, when the new porter came into his office and said:

"I've taken the letter down from the bulletin board, sir, but I just wanted to say that the information you gave me yesterday wasn't quite accurate. Last night, exactly as you warned me I would, I heard the door opening and a few footsteps, but I also clearly heard the voices of two people talking animatedly. This morning, I took down the letter as requested, and I hope you'll forgive me, sir, but purely out of curiosity, I read the letter, and I have to say that not only is it not written by just one ghost, as you gave me to understand yesterday, it is signed by two people. See for yourself."

Mr. Bayo took the letter and read it. And while he read, his face assumed an expression similar to that of the teacher who discovers one day that his pupil has outdone him, and—filled with a strange mixture of envy, pride, and fear—can only wonder in confusion whether, in the future, he will find himself humbled or praised by the person who will, from now on, be the one wielding the power.

Translated from the Spanish by Margaret Jull Costa

Budweiser

THREE FIGURES AND A DOG

By Roberto Ransom

•

To the memory of Javier Oceguera Iturbide,
dear friend and brother

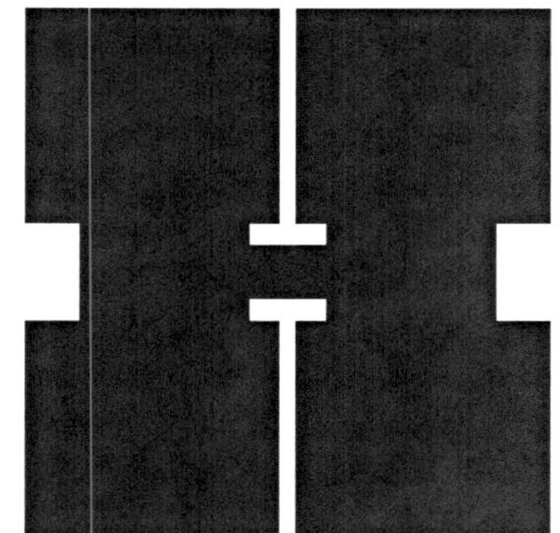e liked to be in the chapel at dawn, and also in the afternoon when something similar, though not identical, occurred. For that to happen, he had to leave home when his wife got up to milk the cow. He'd finally wake himself up by putting his hand into the bucket next to the well and wiping his face. He usually carried a loaf of bread, a piece of onion, and sometimes a little cheese, wrapped in a handkerchief. He'd leave his brushes, pencils, paints, and other tools in a corner of the chapel, behind some stones that hadn't been used during its construction. He didn't paint at that hour. He was waiting for the right color. He'd observe the sky and mix paints in a small clay vessel, smudging them with his finger, measuring quantities, adding water or oil or, on one occasion, wine. He imagined that if the wine was his blood and the blue of the sky he was seeking was the Virgin's color, and the Virgin was his mother and if he and the Virgin were of the same blood, then maybe...

Sometimes the abbot made his rounds to study the painting's progress. At the beginning, he was very patient. After weeks in which the master painter didn't do anything and the wall looked the same, the abbot asked the artist about his method, since he noticed no craft in what he saw. He'd hired him because he knew his work from the time when he still belonged to a workshop in the city. However, because he couldn't count on resources, payment was promised when he finished the painting and, for the very same reason, he hadn't specified a date.

"The craft is over there," said the master painter, pointing toward the cypresses and the sky.

"If you're waiting for it to fall from heaven..." said the abbot and left his sentence unfinished, cutting it off by slowly shaking his head.

"It's not the craft that I'm waiting for, but a certain color. Once I have the color, the figures will simply appear."

"The background means more than the figures to you? Who's ever heard such nonsense! And what are you thinking of painting? Angels, saints... or a color? I've asked you for saints, not a color."

The master didn't say anything now, so he wouldn't further anger the abbot. There would be saints, but those would come later, with that blue as a background—to give them courage, since painted any other way, they'd turn their backs and return to where they came from. He observed the old man for a moment; all in all, even with his wrathful nature, he was a good and wise man.

Facing the respectful silence of the master painter, the abbot said before leaving, "Close your eyes. The images will come to you from here." He touched his chest over his heart with the index and middle fingers of his right hand.

After the sun completely cleared the horizon, the master painter had nothing to do. Since he still hadn't discovered the color, he had breakfast and walked from one end of the chapel to the other, singing softly to warm himself up a little. He lost time in unnecessary ruminations.

With the color, he'd know what he needed to paint, what form to give the saints, everything, but even so, he observed the wall and imagined what he'd fill it with.

He used to return home, to his chores in the country and at the workshop, eat with his wife, and go back to the chapel in the afternoon. He preferred twilight. The blue of May in the great, joyous moments before nightfall had more than once moved him to tears. It seemed like a sign from Heaven, María's cloak, fragrant, pulsating and warm, a passage to another reality whose fleetingness he was grateful for because, had it lasted any longer, it might have led him to something that could turn from ecstasy into terror, something related to death or insanity.

The abbot returned to visit him in the mornings now that his anger had subsided; at most, he'd threaten to look for another painter, even one from another town, to do the fresco. The master painter always responded the same way to him: before the end of summer, he'd have the painting completed. To his wife he'd say that the fresco was progressing and that the abbot was very happy with his work.

Months passed. The wind began blowing differently. The wheat harvest was approaching. The only thing the master painter had done was add more lime to the wall. In his life there was only his wife—two of his daughters had died a long time ago, and two others lived in the city with an uncle, learning everything related to manufacturing and selling cloth—the abbot, and a dog that waited for him on the other side of the bridge to accompany him to the chapel in the morning and return with him at night to the same place. Sometimes he crossed paths with a stranger, or he and Teresa offered lodging to pilgrims; except for that, they lived alone. That's how he wanted it; they could have returned to the city where they'd lived for many years. But he longed for that solitude, he felt it necessary at that moment, and his life revolved around the wall—he returned to the wall time and again, although he hadn't stopped doing other tasks requested of him in his visits to the workshop. He never managed to interest the dog in accompanying him home, and where it came from was a mystery since the painter and his wife had no neighbors for many kilometers around them; besides, it was strange that an animal so small could survive on its own in a region rife with wolves. Furry, with short legs and a big, round head, it wagged what remained of its tail—the other part seemed to have been left in a trap—every time it saw the master painter, although it never barked. The master was the one who spoke, in a loud, untiring voice. On one occasion, it occurred to him that his life was like what he hoped to achieve in his painting: some figures and an enormous blue sky. The blue had to hold the last light of the sun, a yellow as liquid and brilliant as gold. I will paint three figures, he thought one morning, pacing from one side of the chapel to the other as he was followed by the eyes of the dog, who preferred to accompany him that way instead of having to walk. He thought about Teresa, the abbot, and himself.

"I'll include you, too!" he said, looking at the dog and laughing.

The dog wagged its tail.

That day, he painted the dog and didn't return home until it was time to eat. The dog accompanied him on his return to the bridge and remained there. In the afternoon, tired, the master painter considered not returning to the chapel. It would be the first afternoon he didn't do so. He lay down, but after a while didn't feel well and ran to the bridge, promising himself he'd reach the chapel even if only to see the twilight. The dog wasn't on the bridge waiting for him; this saddened him and seemed to suggest something, whether good or bad, he didn't know. He stopped there, looking toward the sun, but night fell swiftly and it was preferable, he thought, not to arrive at the chapel just to get there with the last daylight falling at his back. In the blue instant that transported him, he lowered his gaze to the river, to a spot not so deep where the sandy bottom could be seen. The color of the sky was also there. He realized that he needed dark brown, a bit of black, gold like the sand at the river-bottom in order to be able—together with the mixture he already had—to reproduce the color!

He ran toward home. Everything was happening in a rush. It seemed to him that the stars were moving and that the moon had risen in the sky more quickly than on other nights. He arrived shouting, and half-explained to his wife the cause of his frenzy. She wanted to go with him, but he preferred that she didn't now that he really didn't know what might happen. He collected the necessary things to light the wall, various pigments and oils that he flung in a haversack together with the bread, ham, and grapes, and with the blanket over his shoulder that Teresa had insisted he carry, he left.

He achieved the color, although only with the light of day would he know for sure. He gazed at his palm by the light of the lantern. The wall wasn't large, but preparing it and the paint, combined with applying a thick, even coat, took him many hours. He missed the dog and worked around its figure, taking care to make it appear as if it were painted after the blue. When he finished, he ate with a hearty appetite, feeling great satisfaction. He thought about retuning home, but his desire to see the blue wall when dawn came made him decide to spend the night there. He wrapped himself in the blanket and leaned against the opposite wall, facing the door that he left open so the sun would wake him, without caring if the wolves or some bear entered. He fell asleep planning the figure that he'd begin to paint the next day.

When he woke in the morning, the wall looked like smooth, liquid gold, like water in the well at certain times. The light struck the wall obliquely, so the master painter—whose legs had fallen asleep—dragged himself a few yards over to see it from another angle. A change occurred as the master painter moved along the floor. The gold became blue, the same color as the sky he now saw through the window. There then appeared—it was impossible to know if what he saw had already been there or only became visible because of the glow and the new angle—three figures. They seemed a little frightened, as if they were presenting themselves for the first time.

The master observed them and then began shouting, weeping, speaking like someone possessed, without knowing what he was saying or in what language. They were angels! No. They were saints! No. They looked like men but they also could be women. Two of them seemed more masculine and the other feminine, although the three figures were dressed similarly, with long tunics that covered part of their faces and almost reached their bare feet. The figure on the left had his left arm raised and the other hand held, at the height of his thigh, the fallen hand of the central figure—the woman?—who, with her free hand, grasped her tunic at heart level. The other figure, on the right, clasped his hands on his abdomen and tilted his head gently upward. The three figures looked forward, their legs not together but separated, as if they were walking. The master felt them coming toward him, toward the chapel's interior, toward the world. Where did they come from? He didn't know. He'd tell the abbot that they were emissaries of God. It gave him great pleasure that the color was there, behind them and in front of him, so that he could always look at it, no matter what time of day. He knelt and offered an Our Father and three Hail Marys in thanks and went running to tell Teresa. He wanted her to be the first one to see his blue and the handiwork of God.

• • •

All of it: years of study; months of work; the original discovery, spontaneous and gratifying; the fifth summer workshop for foreigners or nationals interested in art history or in restoration (most attended with the goal of fulfilling a requirement to obtain the master's degree, above all from American universities, so they arrived in Florence for the three summer months when Doctor Giovanni Lombardi was available to accompany them to the Tuscan countryside—it was more like *they* accompanied *him*—and allowed them to observe how he applied his knowledge of fresco restoration on the eastern wall of a small chapel; when they actually did something, it was *exactly* what he asked them to do); his reputation as a specialist in thirteenth- and early fourteenth-century Italian art … in short, the result of his wager, of the passion with which he'd sensed that the stains under the dampness and earth in that chapel were figures, and not just any figures, but the work of a great master, whose skill was displayed in part in the traces of various colors he'd managed to discover (above all a blue and another color, a strange gold like he'd never seen before); from the fourth figure, small and to one side, Lombardi had extracted browns and blacks and, because it seemed to lend itself more to his research, he'd worked more on that one, finally concluding it was a dog; for that reason, when he requested a subvention from the Italian government and from various American universities (it wasn't for nothing that year after year he put up with graduate students, in general individuals forgotten a month after dealing with them and besides that, they irritated him with their terrible Italian, their shallow ideas about art, and their adolescent manners), he'd titled his discovery "Three Figures and a Dog"… all of it would be seen as it truly was the next morning.

The canvas looked like an enormous piece of gauze, smeared beforehand with a solution he'd perfected himself that, in the seventy-two hours it had been hanging, stuck to the fresco as if it were a skin, compressed with an enormous board, should have absorbed, instead of blood, dirt, dust, pollen, flyspecks, incense, saliva, sweat and other kinds of moisture, hair, and the dry skin of generations of pilgrims, everything that wasn't part of the fresco, of the layer of lime, sand, and marble dust, the pigments, and who knows what other ingredients used by the painter at the moment of his creation.

He'd seen enough to be deeply moved. Without being religious, what he'd felt was something that only could be described in religious terms.

They were, without a doubt, human figures, or maybe angels without wings, maybe saints without halos, dressed in the manner of Jews at the time of Christ. This increased Lombardi's interest: medieval painters had no way of knowing what clothing in Biblical Palestine looked like. Speaking of influences—although he preferred not to because he felt as if he were facing something unique—Byzantium and Sicily immediately came to mind, the works of certain monasteries he'd seen in Greece, Bulgaria, and Russia when he was writing his doctoral thesis, much more than Italian art. As with every great work of art, it belonged to its moment, but it also seemed to have fallen out of the sky. It seemed a precursor, dark and almost accidental, of Cimabue and Giotto. The most amazing thing was that everything suggested that the fresco, under the layers that had accumulated with the passing centuries, was perfectly preserved. That, together with the discovery of the colors, had him in a worse state than a father awaiting the birth of his child and, though he tried to hide it, he couldn't sleep, and went several days almost without taking a single bite to eat. He waited anxiously for the dawn.

He was the first one to enter, and it seemed odd to see a dog sitting in the corner. It wagged what was left of its tail and looked at him. Lombardi had never liked animals, but felt obliged to approach it and give it a few pats on the head. Everything was in its place, so it would have been impossible for the dog to have entered—the windows, high in addition to being small and few, two on each side, were all sealed; and the other door, unopened since he'd discovered the place, was closed with its usual padlock. His assistants swore that they hadn't entered the chapel at night after he'd locked it up, or seen the animal before.

"Or it entered before I left and I didn't notice it," thought Giovanni, "or Chris and Laura came here last night and didn't completely close the door."

The tent, big and with individual cots inside, didn't permit the intimacy some students wanted—normally two, one of each sex ... although during the years he'd spent bringing them to this place, that hadn't been the only combination. He'd prohibited his assistants, in no uncertain terms, from entering the chapel at night, given the advanced stage of the work in progress, but it wasn't the first time that they preferred to make love there instead of on the grassy hills under a full moon, at an hour when the weather was most agreeable.

The dog, in the end, was the least of it. They prepared everything to remove the canvas, which looked like an enormous painting stretched over an equally wide frame in such a way that the separation would be uniform when it was pulled with the same effort from all points; for that purpose Giovanni had designed a mechanism with a kind of block, and pulley-wheels fixed to the frame every fifty centimeters, and the central pulley placed at the height of one of the windows, right in the middle of the opposite wall.

The canvas seemed stuck to the fresco, which alarmed Giovanni, but the adhesion lasted only a fraction of a second. When he separated it, Giovanni thought that it was like making a giant photocopy. More to the point, that was his fear. According to his calculations, the liquid should only help absorb the surface material. Still, how could he know—except by chemical analysis, from (incomplete) knowledge of the materials that were used in that era—what was and wasn't on the surface? His solution was, at most, a flip of a coin, even though he might swear that the coin had only one side. He suddenly experienced a phenomenon similar to what he'd felt as a child, when, during a sailing excursion with his family, they'd caught a dorado. The moment they pulled it out of the Caribbean waters, when not only he but also his parents and sister were shouting, for an instant, he'd seen the beauty of the greens, yellows, reds, blues, metallic and slippery, the play between the elements of fire and water (he now recognized the similarity between the blue and gold of the fresco and his childhood memory), before the captain struck the head of the fish with a mallet, causing the colors to immediately take flight, followed all too soon by a grayish hue, like death, settling into its skin. He thought that on this occasion, life hadn't disappeared with spilled blood, but with the vanished colors. For a moment he believed he could see the fresco as it must have been the first time the painter stood back to contemplate it. After his jaw dropped and his hands rose and fell from the emotion of his discovery, he began to scream.

The figures disappeared at the very moment of separation, as if they'd existed between a scab and now-healthy skin. Later, his assistants would say no, they'd seen nothing, nothing except the blue, absolutely stupendous. Imbeciles! Most of them had careers as civil engineers and in order to choose the easiest subjects, meet other young people, and travel, they'd registered for Renaissance Studies, for example.

It wasn't that the blue wasn't stupendous; it was much more than that. By itself, it was worth much more than murals five times its size and infinitely more occupied. Yes, "occupied" was the right word. The way when someone says, "Am I bothering you if I occupy this seat?" However, he'd seen the others. Besides, what would they say about him? He feared that they might see this as a failure. "Your *thinner* worked very well," they'd say ironically. "Your solution has resolved everything." "*Dissolved*," a third one would say. The art magazines would comment on the loss in their editorials, reasoning thus: "With a color like this, what might the painter not have painted?" The tabloids, more sensationalized, would run the headline: "We've gained a color and lost a masterpiece." The tourist guides would show the fresco as what could have been.

He stared at the reverse side of the enormous canvas, seriously doubting he'd find something—what he'd seen wasn't something that could be separated, lifted off with a Kleenex, that could be cleaned with an enormous sanitary pad ("what a strange idea!" he thought)—and, effectively, as he'd later prove in the laboratory, he discovered everything he'd hoped to find—earth, fungi, smoke residues, human skin and eyelashes and other kinds of hair, insect wings, fly specks, and also bat guano—but nothing extraordinary. Now an immense fatalism settled into him. "We've been left without art," he thought out loud.

His assistants tried to lift his spirits.

"*Blue on blue*," said Chris, trying to sound clever.

"Three figures and a dog," murmured Laura.

"Well, for now, there's the dog," said Mónica, the Spaniard, smiling as if to suggest that the matter wasn't so serious, and pointing at the dog that, in fact, continued sitting there.

Translated from the Spanish by Daniel Shapiro

BYZANTIUM

By Ben Stroud

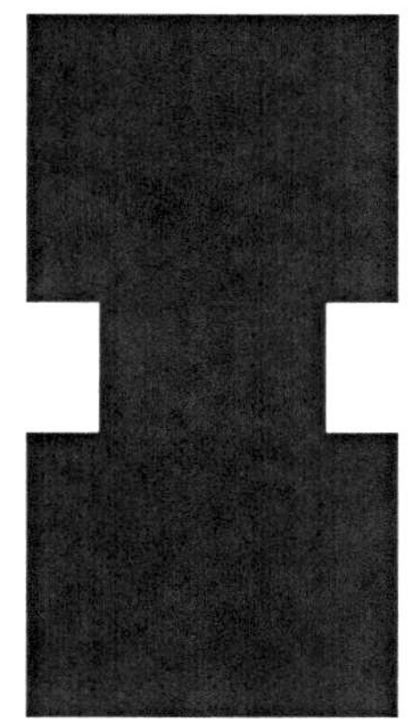 was born a disappointment.

My father was John Lekapenos, one of the Emperor Maurice's favorite generals. He had risen through the ranks from a hovel in Thessaly, and had plans to establish us—through me—among the great families. In the years he waited for my arrival (my mother suffered miscarriages) he elaborated my future career: the army, an illustrious marriage, a governorship or high ministerial position. But when I was finally brought to him, still smeared with my mother's blood, the first thing he saw curling toward him out of the blankets that swaddled me was the chewed red crook of my withered hand.

He must have thought it a talisman in reverse. Not long after my birth, Maurice fell and my father was discharged from the army by his usurper, Phocas. He was forced to leave the camps for good, and, bloated and disheveled, he spent his days sitting in the kitchen with a pot of wine, haranguing the servants about long-ago campaigns against the Avars and the Bulgars. He talked of armies massed in the cold along the Danube, of the legion's priest bringing forth the icon of the Holy Mother, and how he would know, if the sun glinted just right against her eyes, that it would be a good day for fighting. The servants, some of them the children of those same conquered people, ignored him, but I always listened, snug in my hiding spot behind the oil vat, my legs folded against my chest. He loathed the sight of me, would cuff me whenever I came into his presence, but I liked to be near him, and longed to prove myself worthy of his love.

I never had the chance. He died when I was eight. He was in his bedchamber, putting on his old uniform. The Persians had been swallowing provinces whole, the usurper Phocas had in turn been deposed, and my father hoped the new emperor, Heraclios, would give him a legion. They had campaigned together years before, and he'd talked of nothing else for weeks, brightening every time he heard the drums of Heraclios's soldiers as they approached the city. As soon as Heraclios was established in the palace, and Phocas's ashes were tossed in the sea, my father prepared for court. He was to go that morning and was cleaning his sword—this he always insisted on doing himself—when he put his hand over his arm. Then he collapsed. I had hidden myself in a corner behind a chair, and when he fell I stayed there watching for nearly an hour. Eventually I crept away and left him for the servants to find.

That was the end of any hope for us. My mother kept me shut in the city house, where she looked after our dwindling fortune. I spent my days reading or hiding in the garden, listening to the servants' gossip; at my mother's insistence I always wore a specially fitted glove over my hand. I got older, grew restless. When I reached my majority a procuress was consulted and a woman brought to my chamber, and soon after that I began to sleep all day so I could prowl at night. At dusk I would escape through the back entrance to wander the dark streets, going as far as the Hippodrome. There I would watch others taking their pleasure—keeping to the shadows, my hand hidden as I studied a chariot racer leaning into a prostitute, her leg wrapped round his torso, or libertines goading a gilded crocodile in the bearpit, their bodies slurred by powders from the east. When the Persians came and encamped across the Bosporus, laying siege to the city, I went up to the roof every night to watch their attacks and then their slow retreat. When a traitor's body was dragged through the streets I would join the mob, unnoticed, and kick at the corpse and curse it as the chariot pulled it toward the harbor. I had no vocation. I had no life or standing beyond our house's walls. So I lived until my twenty-eighth year, a rattling ghost in the great hive of the city.

• • •

I say until my twenty-eighth year because it was in that year—the first of that brief, confident era following Heraclios's crushing victories against the Persians in the east—that an imperial courier burst into the garden where I was sitting with my mother, drinking tea, and handed me a summons. It came from the Keeper of the Seals, and when my mother saw the purple ink she began to fret. She declared I was to be given some high rank and fussed over my appearance, then decided I was to be executed and began to cry, then reversed herself a dozen times more. I didn't know what to think. The summons itself offered no hints: it only gave directions for when and how I should come to the palace. I was surprised that anyone, much less the Keeper of the Seals, would wish to seek me out. I brushed my mother away and went up to my chamber to spend the rest of the day alone.

When morning came I hired a litter to take me to the Chalke Gate, as instructed. There I showed my summons to the guards, and they admitted me to a courtyard where a large ivy grew. I knew, from one of my father's stories, what I was seeing. The ivy was nurtured from a clipping taken from the old palace at Rome, and the fountain in the courtyard's middle—surmounted by a bronze Romulus and Remus—ran with waters brought from all the empire's corners: the Tiber, the Danube, a spring in Syria, the upper reaches of the Nile. Just beyond the fountain, three men were contesting with an elephant—a spoil from the wars—trying to fit golden covers onto his tusks. A crowd of servants and soldiers had gathered to watch; some had their arms to their noses in imitation of the elephant's trunk, and were whistling, trying to get him to trumpet.

Stacks of crates filled the other side of the courtyard, and it was from behind one of these that a eunuch, spare and with a shaved head, emerged. Squeezing out of his hiding place, he dusted himself off and came up to me and demanded the summons. After he read it he gave me an oddly close look. Then he ordered me out of the litter and took me past the elephant and through a guarded archway. We walked a few steps down a grand corridor of white marble before he stopped and pulled back a tapestry. Behind it, a narrow passageway snaked off into darkness. He went in ahead of me, guiding me by the sleeve, running his other hand along the brick and repeating something to himself. When we came to a tiny iron door he stopped and turned to face me.

"Say nothing," he said. "Stand and wait." Then, twisting and pulling a ring in the door, he opened it and told me to step through.

I had to stoop to clear the topstone, and by the time I stood on the other side, the door had shut behind me. I could barely make it out, its lines fitting smoothly into the wall, but as I looked around me I soon forgot the door. The room glittered with gold. A stream ran through its middle, bound by golden shrubs hung with carnelian fruits, silver briars hooked with thorns. High green trees of mosaic climbed the walls to the ceiling, where light fell from shafts and a sun glided on a circuit. In the center of the ceiling's vault, God stared down, His hair flowing, His eyes gleaming in angry judgment. I knew where I was. I had always thought the Chamber of the Golden Meadow a legend, like the chamber that contained a living map of the sea. I looked again at the silver briars. I had heard it said that some of the thorns were poisoned; only the emperor knew which ones. He would meet his spies and servants here and take them for a stroll alongside the briars. If he grew displeased, he would give his interlocutor a nudge, and the unfortunate's soul would be parted from his body by morning.

The stream trickled, the sun clicked on its track, and I waited, even more uncertain of what was to come.

A half-hour passed, then another. Finally, a door on the far side of the room opened. It wasn't the Keeper of the Seals who stepped through; it was Heraclios himself. The door closed behind him and he took a few steps toward me, then stopped. He was dressed in a simple tunic and a studded leather belt. His beard, grayed by his campaigns, hung below his chest. I stood still as stone—to suddenly be alone with the emperor, this man on whom all the eyes of the known world were fixed!—before it dawned on me that I was to go to him. I did so, bowing two or three times (in my nervousness I forgot the specific demands of protocol), and once I came near he put his hand on my shoulder and looked me over with his fading blue eyes.

"You are Eusebios Lekapenos, John Lekapenos's son?"

"I am," I answered, keeping my head bowed.

"Show me your hand."

He did not specify, but it was not difficult to guess which he meant. I brought my withered hand forward, slipped off the glove, and let him see. He glanced at the bent knobs that were my fingers, the wrinkled crook that was my wrist, then motioned for me to put the glove back on. Then he took me by the arm and led me toward the stream.

“I knew your father,” he said. “We campaigned together. It was a shame that—” He broke off, then nodded at me. After a moment’s silence, he started again, using a falsely conversational tone that, coupled with the unsubtle shift in subject, told me he was getting down to business. With a shiver I realized he was guiding me along the silver briars. “I recall hearing a story that when you were a child you visited several holy men, each of whom promised to heal your hand for you.”

The story was true. Two years after my father died, my mother conceived the notion that a holy man could heal my hand, and she broke our isolation to take me through the streets to find one. Then, as today, holy men flocked to the capital. They set themselves up in the houses of the rich, where they dressed in rags, refused baths, and spat out the delicate morsels offered them at dinner while shouting about fleshpots and the temptations of Babylon. Others, claiming to shun the world, lived in caves or on mountaintops a day’s walk from the city, where they received crowds. And yet others set themselves on pillars in the streets and the fora, shaking their beards at the people below and warning of coming cataclysms.

The first holy man she took me to, chubby and with matted hair, grabbed my hand, put it to his mouth, and licked it. The second made me wait in his cave for two hours while he received other pilgrims, then told me that my hand was twisted because the devil had taken hold of it and that I must repent of my sins. The third spat at me from his pillar, claiming that would be enough, and the fourth told me to fast for six days and then return, by which time, forgetting me, he had left the city. Only with the fifth did I rebel. He had set himself up in one of the grandest houses on the Golden Horn, and promised to heal my hand if I would show my faith in his works by plunging it into a pot of boiling water. I had been given hope, I had believed in them, and when the healings failed I had blamed myself. But as I trembled beneath this holy man’s half-blind stare, his toothless scowl, I understood: He was a charlatan. They were all charlatans. I kicked the pot over, scalding the holy man’s legs, and ran out. The story passed through the city for a week—this I heard from the servants—before dying out. It was painful to recall, and I wondered why the emperor was interested.

“I visited five,” I said.

“And they could do nothing for you,” he said, “except mock your misfortune.”

I didn't know what answer to give, so I remained silent. We reached the end of the stream.

"Have you heard the stories about the monk Theodosios?"

I nodded. Everyone had.

"Let me tell you another," the emperor said as we crossed a footbridge and started walking up the other side. "The Emperor Maurice had a son named Theodosios. He was slaughtered by Phocas alongside his father, but because his head was not sent back to the city, some claimed he had escaped and fled to the Persians for safety." The emperor paused for a moment. He glanced up at the ceiling, to the eyes of God. Then he continued. "That story belongs to the past, and yet only a week ago one of my spies brought me a troubling report. In both Aleppo and Antioch he heard a rumor that Maurice's Theodosios and this monk are the same, and that this monk has a claim to the throne as the rightful heir."

The emperor squeezed my arm, nudged me ever so slightly toward the briars.

"It is a foolish rumor, and yet it disturbs my sleep."

"But, Emperor, surely no one would—"

At a look from Heraclios I quieted. He was at the height of his glory. He had crushed the Persian king Chosroes, regained the eastern provinces, restored the True Cross to Jerusalem, and ordered the golden saddle of the General Shahrbaraz beaten into coins for the poor. It was said that he had saved the empire, and now it would last a thousand more years. Meanwhile, Theodosios was the object of vague stories that had only recently spread to the city. He was a monk at the Monastery of the Five Holy Martyrs, in the desert between Jerusalem and the Dead Sea, and was said to be a master ascetic and to have seen visions of the Holy Mother denouncing the monophysites. He never stirred from his monastery, and as yet, only a few pilgrims from Constantinople had reported seeing him—and they never spoke of the encounter except in the most general terms. The bronze likenesses of his head that merchants sold in the Mese were each unlike the other, because no one knew what he looked like; and his fame paled when compared to that of Father Eustachios, who lived at Mt. Athos and allegedly spoke with the angels, and Severus, an Egyptian who was walking on his knees from Alexandria to Constantinople and stopping only to deliver homilies.

What, I thought, could Heraclios fear from such a man? But then one need only consider his three predecessors: Tiberius Constantine was poisoned, Maurice was made to watch the slaughter of his family before being slaughtered himself, and Phocas was hanged, then burned in the Bronze Bull. It seemed Heraclios had learned that most vital lesson of ruling: for an emperor, natural death is rare. All it takes is for the people to be disappointed—for the corn boats from Alexandria to sink, for the Avars to make unexpected advances on the frontier—and with a single riot, the Christ-Faithful Emperor, Autocrat of all the Romans, can fall. The people only need a candidate to replace him, a candidate much like this monk Theodosios.

"You have led an aimless life," the emperor said once he saw I understood, "a life without meaning, unworthy of your father. I offer you a chance to honor him and to serve the empire. I have need of a man with no fear of holy men, a man not known as one of my spies or assassins, a man who yearns for the glory that has been deprived him." I felt his fingers clench my arm. "I believe I have found this man," he said.

His words sunk like a stone weight. There was no time for consideration. "You have, Emperor," I said.

At that he guided me from the thorns. "I will not forget your service," he said, then touched one of the carnelian berries. The door in the wall opened.

The eunuch was waiting for me. He rushed me back through the narrow passage and whispered hurriedly in my ear. "Do not kill him," he said. "The emperor is superstitious and will not allow the death of a monk. You are to geld him. A eunuch can never hope to be emperor." He flashed me a grim smile, then handed me a knife and a leather purse filled with coins. "You will bring back the fruits of your gelding in the purse. For this the emperor will reward you with rank and gold."

We reached the courtyard just as he finished. Once there, he gave me a shove toward the waiting litter, then disappeared behind the crates. One of the slaves was holding open the litter's curtain, but I didn't climb in. The elephant I had seen when I arrived was now enraged. One of the gold covers had been set on his tusks, but the elephant had crushed the other with his foot and, to the delight of the crowd, was now rising on his hind legs and trumpeting as his caretakers scrambled to tame him. It was a rare spectacle, and even in my state I thought it worth a moment's pause.

When I told my mother the emperor had trusted me with a commission, she fell to her knees and kissed my hem, swearing she would pray each day in the Church of the Holy Wisdom for my success. I fled to my chamber and prepared to leave. I saw no reason to wait. Rather, I was eager to have the thing done. I was rattled from my meeting with Heraclios, and seemed unable to loose the tangle of thoughts that had taken possession of me since our stroll in the Golden Meadow. There was insult: this was an executioner's task, the kind you hire a wretch from the streets to accomplish. And there was fear: where would I begin, how would I bring myself to castrate a man? But twisted amongst these, growing like a summer vine, was pride. At last I could do something worthy, at last I could, in my way, serve the empire like my father. I sailed that very night, using the emperor's gold to buy passage on a Cretan trader, and all during the voyage I stayed in my cabin and practiced. I wrestled with a sack of grain, cut at slabs of meat with the knife. As the ship rocked and the sack lurched, I trained myself to pin it with my lame hand.

My regimen was not perfect—perhaps you find it ridiculous—but by the time I landed at Caesarea I felt I had become, if not expert, adequate to the emperor's task. I purchased three donkeys and spent the day loading them with provisions, then joined a caravan for Jerusalem. Once we reached the city—still in ruins from the Persian occupation—I stopped only to take a meal. Let it be finished, I thought, and that night I hired a guide and set out for the desert.

• • •

I arrived at the Monastery of the Five Holy Martyrs at noon the next day. The monastery, a collection of paths and caves and small stone buildings, lay scattered along the side of a dry ravine, and as soon as I rounded the last bend, a monk came running down from its tower. He intercepted me and introduced himself as Brother Sergios. He was young, just out of boyhood—his pale blue eyes and smooth skin would have caused a stir in the baths—and it was his task, he told me, to aid visitors.

"Where do you come from?" he asked, turning round and walking backward to face me. He had taken the donkeys in hand and was leading me toward the guesthouse, which stood beneath the rest of the monastery on a ledge overlooking the ravine's dry bottom.

"Constantinople," I answered.

"The capital," he said, releasing the two words with a wondered hush. "We don't get many visitors from the capital. The higoumen says it is a pit of devils."

"That may well be so," I said. Brother Sergios laughed, then tied up the donkeys and showed me into the guesthouse. I had to stifle my revulsion. The guesthouse was a long, low edifice of stone and mud. In one large room—the guesthouse's entirety—men slept like hogs, one against the other, while others talked as they ate a sorrowful-looking gruel and played a game with stone pegs. Brother Sergios told me they were a party of farmers, come to pray for their crops, and that the others included a rug merchant and his daughter from Jericho—come to be near Theodosios—and two water-sellers from Bethel who were waiting for one of the monks, a Brother Alexander, to settle a dispute between them.

"There are no other quarters?" I asked.

"No," Brother Sergios said. "Here everyone shares equally."

Fortunately, I had considered this. On the ship I had decided on my plan. I had briefly thought of arriving as a humble supplicant, but felt an aversion to trading on my hand and didn't want to risk the monks presenting me to someone besides Theodosios. Instead, I would arrive as a great personage from court, impressing the rustics to the point that they dare not refuse my requests. I had bought accordingly in Caesarea. The far back corner of the guesthouse was empty and I claimed it. While Brother Sergios swept away the dust, I enlisted two of the farmers to unload the donkeys. On my orders, they cut open the bundles and pulled out carpets and pillows and the unassembled pieces of a chair with ivory facings. I had them hang several of the carpets from the ceiling to form walls and spread another on the floor, along with the cushions, and then fit the chair together and set it in the carpet's middle. I now had a private bedchamber and receiving room as luxurious as one could hope.

I sent the two farmers back to the common room but kept Brother Sergios near me.

"You must be hungry," he said, and indicated a tall earthen pot from which I'd seen some of the others taking their gruel.

"Not for that," I said, then pulled the carpets to and went to my chair, where I struck my best imperial pose. It was taking all my concentration to maintain the act: the whole time, even as I unwrapped a smoked duck stuffed with larks and berries, I kept my withered hand in my tunic. "I shall meet with Theodosios at his convenience," I said.

Brother Sergios shook his head. "Brother Theodosios has taken a vow of solitude," he said. "He meets with no one, unless they are possessed by demons. I believe I'd be correct in guessing you are not so afflicted?"

"I am not," I said, and slipped a piece of the dark duck meat into my mouth.

"Just last week he drove off a demon who had been tempting a brother monk into accidie, and not two weeks before—"

"Tell him I come from the emperor," I said.

Brother Sergios blushed, as if I'd somehow blundered. "Oh, I am not allowed to speak to him," he said. "But I will inform the higoumen."

Brother Sergios left me then, and I continued picking at the duck as I stared out the slit of a window that was my chamber's sole source of light. It faced onto the monastery above, which I now saw was a labyrinth. I had not considered this while preparing myself on the boat, and for a moment I despaired. How would I find, among that maze of paths, that tangle of caves and cells, the man I sought, if no one would take me to him?

• • •

I set this quandary aside—surely, in time, the monastery would unlock itself to me—and decided to make myself more comfortable. I found I had adjusted rather well to my role as the man from Constantinople, and, as my provisions would not last, I hired a goatherd to cook for me. That first night he roasted a kid on a spit. Thinking it wise to win over the other lodgers, once I'd eaten my full I offered the rest of the carcass to them. They rushed forward, all gentleness forgotten as they shoved each other and thrust their grubby fingers at the meat.

After they each had taken a portion, the lodgers fell to laughing and boasting. I retired to my corner to read by my lamp. I was only two lines into the scroll (a farce featuring two Armenian princes) when I heard the rest of the guesthouse suddenly fall silent. My interest piqued, I listened closely, and after several seconds I heard the silence break into mumbled prayers. I stood up and went to the edge of my curtain to see what had happened. A stooped old man, leaning on a cane, his beard nearly sweeping the floor, had entered the room. He was making the sign of the cross over the other lodgers, and when he finished, he started—with a slow, crooked walk—toward me. I left the curtain and returned to my chair. I tried to keep reading, but the words slipped past my mind. All I could hear were the steady, solemn footsteps of the old man.

He entered my quarters, his footsteps muffling as he crossed onto the carpet. I continued my pretense of reading, but that didn't seem to bother him.

"My name is Andrew," he said in a voice more commanding than what I'd expected from one so frail. "I am the higoumen of this monastery."

At that I looked up. "I am honored by your presence," I said. "Would you care to sit?"

"On one of your silk cushions, such cushions that line the halls of Hell, corrupting the body with false comfort?" he answered, spitting as he spoke, his face turning an apoplectic hue. "Bah! Brother Sergios has told me of you. He said a great man had come from Constantinople, to which I now say, by what measure greatness? These carpets, that chair? All such stuff that passes from this earth? They might affect young Brother Sergios, but not me. Better for you to have brought nothing and cleaved to humility."

"If these cushions and carpets offend you, higoumen," I began, but he cut me off.

"Offend me? I do not notice them. I only warn you for your soul. But enough. Tell me why you have come, worldling."

"Very well," I said. "I come at Heraclios's behest. He has heard the stories of Theodosios and has asked me to meet with him in private and investigate their truth."

This last, of course, was my own invention.

"Bah," the higoumen replied, waving his hand at me as if to send me away. "Let the emperor have more faith. Brother Theodosios does not seek fame, nor does he indulge in vanity. He has hidden himself in the mountain so that he may continue his struggle unbothered. Pack up and return to your pit of sin."

"Father Andrew," I said. "I will remain here until I see Theodosios."

"In that case, as you will have much time to yourself, I suggest you take up prayer."

At that he turned and hobbled fast as he could out of my chamber.

There erupted another mumbling of prayers when he reached the common room. Then he left, and I heard a crush and scuffle. I went to the parting in my carpets to look: the lodgers, in rushing toward the kid once more, had toppled the spit.

• • •

The next days passed in frustration. The monks could not force me to leave—they were pledged to hospitality—but neither would they let me see Theodosios. So I tried on my own. Twice I crept up the ravine's side at night to search for his cave, stumbling and slipping as I climbed blindly in the dark; both times I was quickly found and escorted back to the guesthouse. Once I offered three gold solidi to a monk who'd come down to pray with the farmers about their crops; he said nothing, only crossed himself and backed away, as if he'd just had a brush with the devil. Even when I asked about Theodosios—it troubled me that I knew so little about him—the monks shook their heads and shied from me. I only stopped when Brother Sergios explained that Theodosios, in his humility, had asked the other monks to speak of him as little as possible. Five days in, I was certain I had my break. A man arrived complaining of a demon in his tongue. He would be taken to Theodosios, and I need only wait and watch. I spent all day in my quarters, next to the window, pretending to write letters by its light. But the monks came for the man at night, before the moon had risen, and I could see nothing of where they took him.

My efforts were clumsy, and by the end of the week I'd gained nothing. But I learned something in growing up as I had, in longing to be near a father who couldn't stand the sight of me; I learned to notice.

I was bored. My only distraction was to walk up and down the ravine or gamble with one of the lodgers who'd brought dice. Even in the years of my greatest isolation I had been able to talk to the servants, watch the city from the roof, and, when the need took me, drift through the night crowds. A week after I arrived at the monastery, I sent to Jerusalem for an actress. She came the next evening and set up outside the guesthouse. I brought my chair out to sit before her, and the other lodgers came out and reclined along the ledge. We watched as she performed the Rape of Lucretia—she played well the shocked virgin, her hand cupping her mouth—then Leda and the Swan. It was during this last—done with an ingeniously stuffed bird and a skillful gyration of her hips—that I noticed Brother Sergios. Since my attempted wanderings into the monastery, he had been ordered to stay outside the guesthouse. Normally he spent his hours in prayer, eyes hooded as he mumbled and rocked. But when I glanced his way, I saw he'd ceased praying and was watching the actress, who at that moment let fly another startled shout of pleasure.

The next day I sent for a flutist and a dancer, after that, tumblers. I monitored Brother Sergios. Each night he struggled with his prayers, opening one eye, then the other, before giving into the spectacle. He applauded the flutist and his dancer, gasped at the tumblers' tricks. The evening after the tumblers, he asked me about Constantinople, and I told him about the races in the Hippodrome and the painted women in the market, about the ships in the harbor from every sea and the warrens of winding streets that seemed to lead to the ends of the earth. The next night I hired another actress, who acted scenes from the life of the Empress Theodora, then a conjurer who made cups disappear and told fortunes by burning a plucked hair—Brother Sergios had rushed forward, offering one of his own.

It was the clown who came on the sixth evening that proved to be my masterstroke. He juggled firebrands while repeating rhymes about female genitalia. Brother Sergios's laughter echoed up and down the ravine. It must have caught the ears of the higoumen, for the next morning, as I was sitting in my corner of the guesthouse during the hot midday hours, reading, I heard again a hush among the other lodgers and the thump of a walking stick on the stone floor.

"Corrupter!" the higoumen shouted as soon as he passed through the hanging carpets. "Violator! Give up your tricks and leave us!"

"I prefer to stay," I said.

"You are a devil," he said. "I shall cast you out."

"I am a guest, and you are sworn to hospitality. Or have you already forgotten the lesson in the Miracle of the Cisterns, most holy father?" In the Miracle of the Cisterns—one of the more widely repeated wonders of Theodosios—the monks had been punished for putting their own needs above those of their guests.

At my mention of the miracle, the higoumen's face reddened. He raised his stick and held it before him as if he were going to strike me, but after a few seconds he put it down and burst out with a chain of prayers. Then he turned and left without a further word.

That afternoon, Brother Sergios visited me. He bowed and reported that Theodosios had agreed to receive me, and that he, Brother Sergios, would take me to him at nightfall. I sent away the magician who had just arrived and for the rest of the day hid in my quarters.

• • •

I had practiced on the ship, and thoughts of the gelding had weighed ever in the back of my mind, but only now was I confronted with the imminence of my task. Very soon, I would have to cut the flesh of another man, a man I'd not yet even seen. When my father was my age, he'd led a sortie across the Danube and captured an Avar prince. I wondered what he thought about in the hours before setting out. I tried to prepare myself, to ready my mind, to imagine the emperor's wrath, the silver thorns in the Chamber of the Golden Meadow that awaited me if I failed. But nothing worked. I could only wait and hope I acted well when the moment came.

Brother Sergios entered my quarters in the first minutes of dusk. All day he had been absent from his watching post—performing, I imagined, the offices of repentance. He refused to meet my eye, and as he led me up the ravine's side he kept his silence, so I kept mine. I felt for him, but I had my own concerns.

The moon was still down, but the last streak of red remained glowing in the west. We soon passed into a part of the monastery that Brother Sergios was unfamiliar with—at each fork in the trail he had to stop and consult his memory before choosing the way. Pitch-dark caves echoed with the mumble of prayers, and desert creatures, invisible in the darkness, skittered from our path. After a stiff climb we suddenly topped the ravine, the night sky leaping into place all around us. We only stayed a moment, long enough for Brother Sergios to find a new path, marked by a small stack of pebbles, and lead me back down. A few yards in, we crossed a fissure in the rock by a bridge of dried sticks. The bridge squeaked and shifted beneath our weight, and once we were over, Brother Sergios halted and pointed to a far boulder. Its surface flickered with reflected lamplight, the source deep in an unseen hollow. We had arrived.

I stood for a moment, paralyzed. I was here at last, and had to master several flutters of panic. When I finally turned to Brother Sergios, to ask if I should go on, I saw he had gone.

"Come," a voice said, from the same direction as the light. I stepped forward, toward the boulder and into the hollow, which opened into the wide mouth of a grotto. Inside, a monk my age stood with his hands clasped before him. Beside him sat a man weaving a basket, his body made of lumps, his jaw too large for his face. Next to this man was the lamp, and before him lay a reed mat.

"The mat is for you," the monk said.

I couldn't understand—what game was Theodosios playing, having me sit before this unfortunate while he watched? Just as I wondered this, the unfortunate moaned, like a man with an overthick tongue, and the monk said to me, "I ask your indulgence. I wish to finish the basket. Two of the brothers are taking another load to Jerusalem tomorrow."

It took a moment, but, with a prickle of surprise somewhere beneath my gut, I understood. The monstrous imbecile was Theodosios. The other monk was translating for him. Briefly, the thought crossed my mind: was my task necessary? But Heraclios had given his command. Besides, they'd made emperors from worse. I sat and watched as Theodosios wove the basket's rim, twisting and tucking the reed at an expert pace.

He finished the basket, set it aside, then began to moan at me. "I apologize," the monk translated. "I should have received you the moment you came. It was vanity that made me think I could hide myself from the world while others cannot. For this vanity, for this pride, I allowed one of our brothers, whose soul should be my greatest care, to be corrupted."

Theodosios looked at me. I wasn't sure what he wanted, so I said, "For my part, I forgive you."

This seemed to offer him some solace. He smiled crookedly and nodded. He was about to speak again when he stopped and fixed me with a stare. His left eye was not level in his head—it was as if it had been pushed into the raw dough of his face—and it was with this eye that he studied me. He let out a low moan.

"Something troubles you," the monk translated. "Speak."

"There's nothing," I said.

Another low moan. "I know what it is," the monk translated. "I can see it in you."

"I tell you there's nothing," I said, but I rose. I had sent a message to my goatherd to have a horse waiting up the ravine. I could be in the crowds of Jerusalem, disappeared, by noon.

Before I could take a step, Theodosios leaned forward and grabbed my ankle and held me fast. He moaned a long chain of hurried moans. "I see your father in the garden. He's throwing his glass. I see you hiding and weeping and pitying yourself. I see the black knot within you. It was not tied by the devil and it was not tied by God—"

I twisted free. "That is not why I came," I said, struggling to keep my voice from shaking.

Theodosios let out another string of moans. "You may hold onto your pains if you wish," the monk translated. "I have been told your mission. They speak of me in the imperial court and have asked you to investigate my works."

I said nothing, only waited.

"Listen," the monk translated. "I have a message for you to take back. The people and the priests devote themselves to quibbles. They are old women arguing in the market as a flood rises to overtake the city. The emperor is a blind beast, thinking every trembling leaf the tread of a hunter, and he feels not the world shifting beneath him. We are at the gate of perdition. Our sins will be judged, and in these times we must all be brother to one another."

"Proof," I interrupted. "I have come for proof."

And for a moment I believed this was my true mission. Theodosios remained quiet for some time. Then he closed his eyes and mumbled something the monk did not translate. When he finished, the monk—I never would learn his name—went to the back of the grotto and came back with a small jar.

"Give me your broken hand," the monk translated as Theodosios held out his own hand, palm open.

I hesitated. I had not expected this.

"Give me your hand," the monk repeated.

I had no choice. I pulled my hand from my tunic and put it in Theodosios's. With a solemn nod he sent the translator away, then peeled off the glove and poured ointment from the jar and began rubbing it into my skin. For ten minutes, he kissed the crook of my wrist, the knobs of my fingers. He scrubbed my hand with his hair, and the whole time moaned prayers. I watched his face and I watched my hand. When he ceased his efforts it remained withered as ever.

Theodosios studied my hand, his already misshapen face contorted in bafflement. He looked up to the grotto's ceiling, moaned something, then rubbed more ointment into my fingers and wrist. He signed for me to wait and tried to communicate, with moans and shaking head, that he didn't understand. But I did. I saw again the holy men who had humiliated me in my youth: their hollow smiles, their empty promises, their mocking eyes. Here was another with his finely honed act, playing me for a fool. It seemed Heraclios knew well what he was doing when he chose me. I burned with shame—for a moment Theodosios had gotten to me—and I felt no hesitation now.

Before he could take my hand again, I leapt onto Theodosios and pinned him with my knees. He moaned; I covered his mouth with my good hand. He struggled, pulling himself up; I shoved him back to the grotto's floor. With a jerk, I forced up his habit, then felt in my tunic for the knife, squeezing its handle between my stunted fingers. He was screaming and struggling. I had no time. Taking my other hand from his mouth, I gave him a cuff to quiet him and grabbed his testicles, lifting them from his body, and made the cut. With a single tug the knife sliced cleanly through the boneless flesh and it was done. Theodosios twisted beneath me, his bellowing mouth bent in a terrible grimace, but I felt a quiver of calm relief—it hadn't been nearly as hard as I'd feared.

The other monk had reappeared in the grotto's entrance, panting and silent, in shock, and I was recalled to my senses. I stuffed Theodosios's testicles in the leather purse and pushed my way out. Once across the footbridge, I fled blindly, but fleeing was easy. The monastery was only a labyrinth when you were looking for someone, not when you were running away. I slipped and slid on the paths, shoving my way through the monks who'd come from their caves at the sound of Theodosios's howls. By the time I made it to the bottom of the ravine, they were sounding the monastery's wooden bell. Its furious *tock* filled the valley. I skirted the guesthouse—the lodgers had emptied out onto the ledge—and ran to where the goatherd was waiting with the horse.

"Sir," he said as he helped me up. "What's happened, why are they ringing the bell?"

"Don't worry yourself about that," I said.

He was still holding the reins when he pulled back and pointed. "Sir," he said, "your hand."

I looked down. It was ribboned with blood. But there was something else. I gave the goatherd a kick, took the reins, and spurred the horse. I soon lost track of where I was going—I was too startled to think, and kept looking in disbelief at my hand. The goatherd had not seen what I had seen. He had seen only the blood. I saw something more. Where the blood had run over my hand, it had made the withered flesh whole.

• • •

I passed the next day in a baffled, wandering stupor. I am still uncertain how I made it out of the desert. As I sat upon my horse, a lightness coursed through my veins. My mind reeled: Each explanation I could fathom crumbled in the face of another. He knew; he didn't know. He was a true holy man; it was some sort of new charlatan's trick. And at the same time, I felt a sickness for what I had done. But then I would look at my hand. I had washed it and wiped it clean, and as my horse ambled and nibbled at dry grass, I gazed at its new perfection. I flexed its fingers, traced the straightened, flat pan of its palm. I held both hands side by side. They were mirrors of each other, though the healed hand was smoother, pinker.

Just before sunset, I reached the orchards outside Jerusalem. I rode round the city and headed straight to the coast. I imagined the new life that awaited me: a place in court, prominent seats in the Hippodrome, our family restored to its rightful place. Perhaps it wouldn't be too late for me to take a command, some squadron on the Dalmatian frontier. If any asked about my hand, I would say I had visited a sulfur spring in Greece and was treated by a physician. But surely few would ask: I was unknown. Only the emperor's long-memoried informants had any idea who I was. That, I decided, would soon be changed.

• • •

By the time I returned to Constantinople, I had regained enough of my reason to be fearful. I didn't know what news had reached the city, or what the reaction might be: perhaps mobs filled the fora, clamoring for my death. Once off the boat, I hid in the crowds and gleaned the conversations of passersby. I trailed parties of beggars through the markets, sat with the mad outside church doors. Only among these did I feel safe, unseen. Within hours of my arrival, while huddling outside the Church of the Holy Wisdom with a pair of moaners, I heard the first rumors of the gelding. Some passing monks were discussing it, and I was relieved: they had the story wrong. "The assassin was a monophysite," one declared, setting the others off. "No, I heard he was a Jew," "No, a devil," "He had Theodosios by the throat and meant to destroy him," "Satan was testing him," "God intervened," "No, it was a punishment, for pride." The monks all frowned, though on one I detected a stifled smile. By evening, a troupe of clowns had spread through the city, portraying the surprised Theodosios and his veiled attacker.

After another day of listening, satisfied I wasn't hunted, I made my way to the Chalke Gate, where I whispered my presence to one of the guards. I was expected: within a minute, the eunuch from before came and showed me directly to the Chamber of the Golden Meadow. There I knelt and waited, nervous, every organ beneath my chest grown cold, my palms and my scalp beading with sweat. I returned triumphant, but what if Heraclios had lied to me, what if my reward awaited me here, among the silver thorns? I glanced at them now, wishing I knew which were poison-tipped.

I had just begun counting the drops of sweat falling from my forehead when the emperor burst through the door and strode toward me, roaring gleefully. "I have heard the reports!" he said. "There'll be no more talk of a monk on the throne." He stood over me and beamed.

I kept my head bowed. Warm relief flooded through me. My fears now seemed groundless.

"Your father would be pleased," Heraclios went on. "You have done your duty." Then he chuckled and seemed to play out the gelding in his mind, for I saw him make a flick of the wrist like a man slicing grapes from a vine. After two more of these flicks, he asked, "Do you have them?"

I bowed lower and offered up the leather purse, which I had kept tied to my tunic since fleeing the monastery. Before leading me to the Chamber, the eunuch had made sure I remembered to bring Theodosios's testicles: it seemed Heraclios possessed a cabinet near his bed in which he stored, preserved in vinegar, similar artifacts taken from vanquished pretenders and Persian generals, among others.

"Tell me," the emperor said when he finished prodding the purse, "did he squeal?"

"He screamed in pain, emperor," I answered, speaking as evenly as I could.

"Very good. That is all. You may go," the emperor said.

I hesitated. I felt as if I couldn't move and before I knew what I was doing I called out, "Emperor." He looked back—he had already stepped toward his door—and I held up my bared hand.

The stream purled beneath the silver briars. Above us the eyes of God stared, fixed in stone and gilded glass.

"Theodosios?" Heraclios asked, his face gone pale.

I nodded.

The emperor came to where I was kneeling. He grabbed me by the wrist and examined my hand. "So he was genuine," he said. "That is unfortunate."

I quaked. On the ship back, as my fascination with my hand settled into calm acceptance, doubts began to plague me. Surely I had committed a grievous crime. Now I was certain I would be tipped into the briars.

"I will tell you something," the emperor said. "It is by far not the worst thing I have had done." I waited for the shove, for the prick of the thorns, but before I could close my eyes he let me go, pressed the carnelian berry, and sent me away.

• • •

Released from the Chalke Gate, I picked my way through the Mese's undulant, squabbling crowd of merchants. Dazed still from my meeting with Heraclios, I paid no attention to the clothier who thrust a wool mantle into my hands, or to the tin seller who danced before me, his cups dangling from his arms. I was headed, at last, for home.

"Eusebios," my mother said when I stepped into the courtyard. She stood there as if knocked still, whispered a veneration to the Holy Mother, then clutched me and wept into my shoulder. My heart—this surprised me—swelled, and for a moment I forgot all that I had done. Only when she pulled away did she see my hand.

"How?" she asked, seizing it and pulling it close to her eyes.

I started on about a Grecian spring, and she scoffed. So I told her the truth, and in the telling I felt suddenly proud. What I had done was difficult. I had served the emperor. And mightn't I have received a sign that I had done right? But before I could finish, my mother dropped my hand.

"That was you?" she said, backing away from me. Her flesh seemed to have turned ashen. "You have mocked God," she pronounced. "That hand is a curse. He has shown you His power." She looked at me, her face stricken with disappointment, then fled from the courtyard to her room, where she shut herself for the rest of the afternoon.

For several days after, she avoided me. Then one morning, a servant came to my bedchamber as I was dressing and presented me with a new glove. I didn't need to ask who had sent it. I wanted to throw it across the room; I wanted to send it back torn. But I put it on. When I went down, my mother was waiting in the courtyard. With a brief flick of her eyes she confirmed the glove's presence. After that, she never again mentioned my hand.

• • •

I was now a great man. I rode through the city, shouting across the rabble to other young courtiers I had met, and involved myself in Hippodrome politics, supporting the Blues, as my father had, and standing feasts for the chariot racers. Heraclios had kept his promise of reward. It had been announced that at the Feast of Palms I would be granted an income and sub-patrician rank, which, among other privileges, would allow me a title, the use of blue ink, and the right to be drawn in a carriage by four brown ponies.

A month after my return, I received perhaps my greatest honor: an invitation to dine at an imperial banquet in the Triclinium of the Nineteen Couches. I sent for the tailor and commissioned a new tunic, and when the evening came I daubed myself with scent. As I was leaving, I could hear my mother in her room, murmuring her constant prayers. I ignored them, and once I stepped in my litter I slipped off my glove and tossed it to a servant. At the dinner I was given a poor seat, far from Heraclios—a hundred men separated us—and near the customary twelve paupers. But I was there. I belonged. The musicians played airy tunes, the tableware glittered in the lamplight, and the emperor, I was certain, had looked at me with approval.

It was when the wine was being poured and I had begun talking to the youth on my right—the son of a Bithynian tax-farmer—that one of the paupers, seated toward the middle of their table, leapt up and hissed at me. I had noticed him giving me twitchy glances and had hoped it would end there. His beard was matted, his skin burnt to leather, and after he hissed again he pointed at me with a pheasant bone and shouted, "Blood on his hand!" The entire room fell silent and stared. I sat as still as I could. That was my defense. I felt each pulse's tremble. Someone seemed to be squeezing my chest, denying me all but the tiniest spoonfuls of breath.

Over the last days, the rumors about the events at the Monastery of the Five Holy Martyrs had grown accurate. My name had been mentioned, as had the changed state of my hand. I had not been as forgotten as I'd thought. The day before, I had found a priest waiting outside my door, begging for a moment of my time to question me and inspect my hand, and several times I had noticed my litter being trailed by a scattering of curious idlers. There was vigorous debate—Why had I been sent? What did the miracle mean?—but none had confronted me openly. I enjoyed the emperor's favor, and I had hoped that soon all such attentions would disappear.

Finally, a soldier pulled the pauper from where he stood and the next dish, turtles cooked in their shells, was brought out. Everyone returned to their conversations as if nothing had happened: they were all well-practiced courtiers. The Bithynian began rattling on about some gossip he'd heard concerning the Greens' new bearkeeper, and at the next table a general from the east assured his neighbors that the recent Saracen unrest would be put down by winter. But I couldn't return so easily. The latest report held that Theodosios had retreated further into the desert, and since that night there had been no new miracles. I saw again his twisted face, heard his cries, felt his bloody manhood in my palm. I thought of what my mother had said. A curse.

The musicians changed songs. A slave reached over my shoulder and pulled apart my turtle shell. I reminded myself that I had served an empire that would last forever, that I had become the son my father died wanting. I hid my hand under the table. This was my arrival. I had the rest of my life to work the intricate ratios of regret.

THE BASTARD

By Patrick deWitt

The Bastard approached the farmhouse on foot, a leather satchel in one hand and a long stick of pine in the other. The sun had dropped behind the mountains, and the heavy evening cold came hurrying into the valley. He watched the smoke spinning from the stone chimney and felt a passionate loathing for every living thing; he spit a slug of mucous over his shoulder and muttered the third-rudest word he knew. Shaking this feeling away, or secreting it, he stepped up the walk to the front door where he was met by the farmer, red-nosed Wilson, who spoke before the Bastard could open his mouth: "There's no work for you here, not even half a day." This was just the opposite of what the Bastard had hoped to hear, and it took no small effort to conceal his disappointment, but his recovery was swift, and without a moment wasted he launched into his performance.

"You misunderstand me, sir. I am merely passing by and was hopeful for a bed of hay to lie down upon. I have my own food to eat, and shall require nothing from your household other than a splash of water in the morning, but then I will be on my way, and you will hear nothing of me for the rest of your days. Of course, I will be sure and make comments to all those I pass on my way out of town regarding the good farmer Wilson's hospitality, his generosity, his sympathy for those working to make their way in life. Mark my words, they will learn all about it!"

Wilson was caught off guard by the stranger's speech, and he shifted back and forth in his boots, scratching his eye—the actual eyeball, which itched devilishly and was forever bloodshot. "How'd you know my name?" he asked.

The Bastard blinked in disbelief. "Your name, sir? But doesn't everyone in this area know your name? Are you not well-thought-of hereabouts? Is it not understood that you are the most hard-working farmer, the most clever and able?" He threw back his head and laughed. "How did I know his name, he asks me! That's modesty for you."

At this, the tension gripping the farmer's body uncoiled itself, and all his mistrust fell away. Now he stood in his doorway, vulnerable as a calf, and the Bastard knew the bed of hay and jug of water were his for the taking. Only he had no plans to settle for this humble victory, and when the farmer acquiesced, pointing his crooked thumb at the barn, the Bastard did not simply bow and step away, but pretended to stumble, and in doing so gave his satchel a tap with the toe of his boot. This brought forth the clink of a bottle, muffled but unmistakable, and he watched the farmer's expression with all of his concentration. When Wilson shuddered and twitched, the Bastard knew he had the man in his clutches. *Look at him,* he thought. *He wants a drink so badly his pores are yawning open.* He imagined each of Wilson's pores as a tiny mouth, each with a miniature pink tongue sticking greedily out in hopes of catching a splash of whatever the bottle held. This nearly made him laugh, but he collected himself and returned to the role of deferential outsider:

"Before I make my bed down, it would be an honor if I might offer you a short drink of rye whiskey. I've got a full and unopened bottle, a gift from a friend, only I don't care all that much for spirits. Frankly, I find they upset my constitution. But you, sir, look all the more hearty than I. Perhaps you take the rare drink?"

Wilson could scarcely believe his luck. He looked here and there into the expanse, a frightened expression on his face as though he expected some vindictive God or another to swoop from the sky and steal away the magical passerby, rye whiskey and all. Witnessing this reaction, it was all the Bastard could do not to strike the gluttonous farmer to the ground. How he longed to grind his boot-heel into the man's sickening face! "Please accept," he implored, "otherwise you will wound me deeply. And really, isn't it the least I could do, considering the kindness you've extended to me?"

So it was that the Bastard was admitted into the house itself. Wilson rushed to fetch two mugs, and lay these on the kitchen table; his hand trembled as he fell to drinking the precious rye with much slurping and heavy breathing. When there came the uncertain rhythm of dainty footsteps at the top of the stairs, the Bastard made his innocent query: "Is that your wife, sir? I would be honored to meet her. What a lucky lady, to spend her days in this grand home, and with such a gentleman as yourself at her side."

You're overdoing it, the Bastard told himself. But Wilson was distracted by his rye-guzzling, and his guard was down. "That's my daughter," he said. "Wife died seven months ago."

"Daughter?" said the Bastard. "Is that so? Hmm, yes."

But of course he knew about the daughter already. Here was the reason he had come to Wilson's home in the first place. Here was the reason he had stolen the rye from the general store, and why he plied the farmer so generously while he himself abstained. When the daughter, still hidden, began to hum and sing, the Bastard broke character, and a wicked smile spread across his face. Wilson was already quite drunk, but through the haze he saw this smile, and found himself distantly concerned. Pointing at his guest, he slurred, "You, now. Wait a minute."

"Drink up," snapped the Bastard, "that's all you want anyway, isn't that right?"

Wilson cast his eyes down, impotent, scolded. Ducking his face to the mug, he snuffled like a hound, inhaling the rye's burning fumes. He was simultaneously very glad and very sad.

• • •

Earlier in the day, the Bastard entered a feed store five miles to the east of Wilson's farm. The clerk's face was a broad purple depression with eyes and teeth dropped in, and he looked as though he had no bones in his body whatsoever—a gelatinous mass of blubber and grease-slick flesh. As such, the Bastard despised him on sight, for if there was one thing he had no tolerance for, it was the overweight. He greeted the clerk thusly: "Hello, my good man! Shaping up to be a fine day out there."

"What'll it be," the clerk intoned, staring at the floor and chewing lazily. An unfriendly sort, but the Bastard had gone up against many a more formidable foe than this pellet salesman, and he kept his disgust well-buried.

"I wonder, sir," he said, "if you might help me locate an acquaintance of mine."

"A *what* of yours?"

"A friend," he explained. "Or not quite a friend, but someone I met that I should like to visit with again. It was just outside your store, in the road there. He was a farmer, if I'm not mistaken."

"Lotta farmers around here. Fact, that's all there is. What's his name, did you say?"

"Here now, we've arrived at the root of my problem. I never caught his name. But, I was thinking, perhaps if I were to describe him?"

The clerk said nothing. It seemed he was chewing on his own tongue.

"Hmm," said the Bastard. "Yes, well, he was a working fellow, much like yourself."

"You saying he looked like me?"

"Not terribly like you, no. But in the general sense, there was some similarity."

"Mister, did he look like me or not?"

"He had a daughter with him," said the Bastard. "A young woman."

"All right. And what's *she* look like?"

The delicate Bastard was prepared for just this question. He held his hand out to exhibit the golden wedding band on his ring finger. Speaking lowly, in confidence, he said, "I myself am already engaged to be married, and I fear that, since meeting my beloved, I have a habit of altogether ignoring the fairer sex."

A customer entered the store and began walking the aisles with a hand truck. Peering over the Bastard's shoulder, the clerk said, "You saying you saw the daughter or didn't you?"

"What if you were to describe her? That is, describe some of the farmers' daughters?"

The clerk groaned in annoyance, and the Bastard sensed he had used up every ounce of the man's charity. Wordlessly, then, he lay a single bill onto the countertop. The clerk was unsurprised by this; he retrieved the money and stuffed it away, looking all the more accommodating, or at least not quite so hostile as before. "Okay, let's see. There's Lund's girl. She's about fifteen, ugly as a hedge fence, dog breath."

"That doesn't sound right, no."

"Well, what about Miller's girl, Sandy? Twelve years old, maybe. Coke-bottle glasses. Got a brace on her leg."

The Bastard shook his head. "This was a young *woman*. And though I only glanced at her in passing, I seem to recall, if I may speak frankly—well, she was somewhat fair."

"Mister," said the clerk, "there ain't no *fair young women* in these parts."

The words settled in, and the Bastard wondered if there wasn't some way he might get his money back. But no, the town was a wash—it had happened before—and he stepped back from the counter, automatically thanking the clerk and moving to the exit. Halfway to the door, however, the customer that had entered a moment earlier spoke to the Bastard from the far side of the store. "Could be Wilson's girl you're thinking of."

The Bastard turned slowly. "Wilson," he said.

The customer nodded. "My sister does their washing? Told me Wilson's daughter's shaping up to be a prize beauty. Blonde and fair, just like you mentioned."

"Wilson hasn't hardly set foot in town since his wife died," the clerk said skeptically.

"A widower," said the Bastard. "Yes, that sounds familiar."

The customer said, "Sister says old man Wilson won't let the girl out of the house. On account of how she looks I mean? Don't seem right to me, but I'm not surprised, the way that man drinks. Well, what can you say about it?"

"Wilson," said the Bastard. "Yes, it's all coming back to me now." Of the clerk, he asked, "Where can I buy a bottle of whiskey?"

"Three down from here," the clerk answered, pointing.

"And which way is it to Wilson's farm?"

In the general store he dropped a lit match into a paper-filled trash can, and while customers and employees swarmed to bat at the flames he made off handily with the rye. He felt joyful as he left the town, forging ahead into the open spaces, the farmland. *All or nothing,* he thought, decapitating flowers with his stick of pine. *Otherwise, what's the point?*

• • •

Wilson lay face down on the table, a void where only minutes earlier there was a man, or half a man. The Bastard wrenched the mug from the drunkard's claw and returned the rye to the bottle. There was enough left to poison the farmer once more, perhaps twice. And after this, then what? *I don't know, and I can't care,* he thought. He had never been one to fret about the future. He stood and stepped further into the room, taking in his new surroundings with his hands behind his back, like a man luxuriating in a museum or rose garden. Each time this crucial maneuver of entering a home was accomplished, he was struck by the image that a house was, after all, much like a human skull.

The furnishings were unremarkable: candles, lace, quilting, and wicker. It had probably been a comfortable enough space before Wilson's wife had died, but now it was bleak, dark—a sink full of grime-coated dinner plates greeted the Bastard as he stepped into the kitchen. The sight of it reminded him of something the helpful feed store customer had said, that his sister did Wilson's washing. But why was this so, with the daughter in the house? Why was everything so dingy? This only made him all the more curious about the girl, and his head began to pound as he imagined her alone in her room. He thought, *She's let everything go to hell, while her father savors a slow death.* He walked to the base of the stairs and kicked the tread with his heel. "Girl," he called. "You up there, girl." There came a gasp from the darkness above him, and the Bastard thought almost fondly of her paper-drumming mouse-heart. He returned to the kitchen and rolled up his sleeves. He had elected to clean the plates and cutlery himself, not to curry favor with his newest acquaintances, but because the very thought of their laziness filled him with an anger whose insistence was frightening to him.

• • •

They pulled Wilson up the stairs and installed him in his vinegary, scooped-out bed. The daughter stood panting and looking sadly down at her father. Her dainty hands rested atop the curve of her hips; the Bastard could not help but stare at the yellowing bruises on her otherwise pale and fine forearms and wrists. She noticed his noticing and pulled down the sleeves of her blouse. She was absolutely beautiful, it was true.

"Who are you?" she asked.

"No one, yet. I struck up a conversation with your father and he invited me in."

She pondered the words. "My father does not strike up conversations."

"Anyway, we spoke."

"What did you give him to drink?"

"Rye."

Her face tightened. "You must never give him any more."

"Why is that?"

By way of answering, she merely pointed at her father; and it was a thoughtful reply when the Bastard considered the farmer's sorry state: his inhalations were stilted, his exhalations rasping, a high whine sounding over top of the gurgling lower tones emanating from the back of his throat. It was an unpleasant thing to witness, and the Bastard thought the man could die at any given point. The anger from moments earlier revisited him and he asked the daughter, "But who are you to say what I should and shouldn't do?"

"Who are you at all?" she asked.

"I've just told you I am no one."

"And yet here you stand, flesh and blood, you've kicked my stairs and upset my reading. You've poisoned my father and spoiled any chance he'll lift a finger in the morning. If you are no one, sir, I should never like to meet someone, for what might he bring but utter ruin!"

The Bastard was opening his mouth to call the girl the second-rudest word he knew—it was forming in the basin at the center of his tongue—when suddenly the lone window in the farmer's room flew open and a gust of cold wind swarmed them, ruffling their clothing and hair. The daughter rushed to close the latch, acting very much put-out, even embarrassed by the wind; the Bastard, on the other hand, was struck with a sudden good humor at the interruption, and by the time the daughter turned back, he was stifling laughter. Just the moment she noticed this, she too began to laugh. It was as though the fresh air and the loud rap of the pane hitting the wall, which had made them both jump, had cleaned away their independent worries, and now they stood together, partnered in a wholesome adventure. She returned to stand over Wilson and asked the Bastard, "Will you help me take his clothes off?"

"No, I won't!"

They laughed again, and long after the laughter died, a smile clung stubbornly to the daughter's lips. She found herself stealing glances at the stranger, her blue eyes darting in the candlelight. It is late to mention it, but the Bastard was terrifically, probably unfairly handsome.

"What is your name?" he asked.

"My name is Molly. What is your name?"

"Molly."

"Your name is Molly?"

"*Your* name is Molly. Molly, Molly."

"Will you tell me your name or won't you?"

"Molly," said the Bastard, dreamily.

Wait now, he did help her disrobe Wilson after all, peeling away the damp socks, the stained pullover, the canvas pants, stiff from dried mud and muck. The farmer's naked person was bordering on the macabre. It was like an exhibit people might pay a small fee to look over and afterwards feel exhausted by. His penis was tiny and thin, the hood chapped and wrinkled; the Bastard reached out and flicked the tip. Scowling, Molly asked him not to touch her father.

"That, and don't give him any rye," he said.

"You think I'm making a joke, but another dose of alcohol might kill him."

"Here is the most interesting statement I've heard in hundreds of hours."

Molly, cautiously: "Why won't you tell me your name?"

But the Bastard was distracted by the odors Wilson was now sharing with the room. He hadn't noticed at first, but all at once it was as though a pair of black-smoke hands had him gripped about the throat. Molly, too, could not ignore the stench. They turned longingly to the window. "O, fickle wind," said the Bastard, "will you never push when I wish you to push?"

Molly laughed a third time; the Bastard, not at all. Her gladness dried up at once, and what remained was confusion, also a vague lust—but mainly confusion. Who was this person in her home? What were his plans? And if she found these untoward, what might she do to prevent him from seeing them through? She had not spoken with anyone other than her father in so many days and nights. "Come away," she said. "I will see you out."

Now the Bastard laughed.

They moved downstairs to sit together and drink weak tea. The Bastard said, "I expect your man will be by soon enough, and that he will wish to strike me down for my impertinence and forcefulness."

"Oh, no," said Molly.

"He is traveling, is that it?"

"He is not…" She shook her head. "There is no he."

"He hasn't died?"

"There is no one," she answered tiredly. "There is never anyone."

"Of course," said the Bastard. "Yes, now I can see that. For if there were a man, you would not have those marks on your wrists and arms. If I were yours, there wouldn't be."

Molly watched him. Pointing at the golden band, she asked, "But why do you speak like this, when you are already another woman's man?"

"What? Oh, this." He had forgotten he was wearing the ring. He thought back to the man he had stolen it from, how fat he had been, how difficult it had been to remove. He pulled the band from his finger and pushed it across the table. Puzzled, she took it up and studied it politely. When she pushed it back, he returned it to her.

"What?"

"Put it on."

"Why?"

"Because I love you."

A flush of blood to her cheek and breast, and the Bastard became hugely engorged under the table. Later, after the re-opening of the rye, they fell to the floor before the stove and consummated a mutual admiration, which even for the Bastard was part-way genuine. After she had fallen asleep, he stayed awake a long while, looking out the high window at the stars in the sky. His mind was an illuminated scrim with nothing at all behind it.

• • •

The next morning, Wilson staggered down the stairs, a dedicated pain clamping his brain and eyes and teeth. As such, he was in a foul mood *before* he found his daughter and the Bastard wrapped in a naked embrace on the ground. He paced awhile, then removed his shotgun from the wall. The muzzle was cold against the Bastard's chest; when he gasped, Molly awoke, speaking calmly, sanely: "But Father, you mustn't. We're to be married." She pointed at the field of wheat behind the farmhouse. "There," she said. The Bastard and Wilson both squinted to look.

• • •

The Bastard was happy all that week, and he fell into the wedding preparations with an atypical enthusiasm. Riding Wilson's horse into town, he introduced himself to the dressmaker and tailor, the baker, the butcher, the priest, the jeweler, and grocer, explaining to all his predicament, which was this: despite his already being engaged to another, he had fallen quite unexpectedly and hopelessly in love with Molly Wilson, and they were to be married that very Sunday, as per her wishes. Of course, as everyone in town knew, Molly's father had no money to speak of, and his meager crops could not be harvested for many weeks.

But no matter, the Bastard had sent a letter to his bank in N_______, with instructions to empty his account and remit the balance just as soon as they were able. He admitted this was no pittance, and that, truth be told, he might pay for ten weddings one after the other and not lose so much as a moment's sleep worrying about the expense. But, he explained, the bank could not be expected to return him his funds in so short a time, which was why he was now forced to throw himself upon the township's mercy and request a line of credit. At the start, this went poorly, and he was rejected by all. When he returned the next day with the lovely Molly at his side, however, the vendors found themselves all the more inclined to assist this charming young couple, so clearly enamored of one another, and at last the Bastard's every wish for the most lavish celebration was granted, and without a single penny paid out in advance.

The times they were not preparing for the wedding and making plans for their future, Molly and the Bastard were consummating. They consummated in every room in the house, including her father's. They consummated in the barn, in the loft, in the stalls, and even in the wheat fields, hunched over like animals. Molly was an excellent consummator. The Bastard was surprised. *You never can tell,* he thought. The wedding drew near and there was virtually no chance she was not pregnant, which pleased him. Wilson, for his part, lay immobile most every day. The Bastard had had several cases of ale delivered to keep the old man quiet, which proved a shrewd and effective measure.

The Bastard inspected the stage that had been erected by town carpenters in the field behind the farmhouse. It was Sunday morning, just after dawn, and as he stepped about in the wheat he was struck by how cold it was on the ground, while at the level of his hip, where the sun poured over the top of the wheat, it was pleasingly warm. He climbed the stage staircase and walked along the sturdy boards. Standing in the very center, where he was to be married, he brought down his heel as hard as he might, but there was not a bow, not so much as a creak from the structure. The carpenters had been unhappy about working on credit, but they hadn't shirked their work, and the Bastard admired them for it. He dragged his toe back and forth across the lumber, enjoying the sound the sawdust made as he ground it down. A wind came along and spun the dust in dizzy circles, then pulled it clear off the lip of the stage, scattering it over the crop. Looking up, he saw Molly standing in the kitchen window, beaming at him. He smiled and waved. He had a stick of wheat in his mouth. He felt jaunty.

Every inhabitant of the town stood before the stage, mingling and shaking hands, passing time with pleasantries and gossip. The weather was suited perfectly to the event and there was not a woman in the crowd that didn't feel a twinge of envy, for all was picturesque, and the romance of Molly and the Bastard had become legendary:

"Oh, but his manners are so fine."

"And did you see how pleased she looks?"

"She is positively glowing."

"But who can blame her?"

"I understand he's quite rich."

Molly watched her guests from behind the curtain in her bedroom. The dressmaker was putting the finishing touches to the hem, but there was no rush or worry, and the bride-to-be felt serene and peaceful. There came a knock on the door and Wilson stepped in, hat in his hand. He wore a suit, and his hair was combed down and parted, his beard was trimmed, and he stood humbly, soberly before his daughter. When he spoke, his throat was choked with emotion.

"I want to tell you how pleased I am today, Molly. I know I've been a wretch to live with ever since your mother passed, with my drinking and mourning and carrying on. But I swear to you, from this point forward I am born anew. I will go back to being the man I once was, the man that raised you, a decent man, worthy of your love, and the love and respect of your husband and children." He broke off, and Molly crossed the room to hold him. They were both in tears, as was the dressmaker. Wilson stood back, nodding, wiping his eyes and cheek. As he made his way to the door, he said the priest had arrived, and the guests were becoming restless. Molly asked after her beloved, and Wilson answered he had taken out the horse, to clear his mind he had said, but would be back any moment. He was wearing his new suit of clothes, Wilson told her, and he looked the picture of pride and prosperity.

Taken out the horse? Molly thought. She found this puzzling, troubling even, but then she often found him so. He was a mystery to her, sure enough. How queerly he watched her when they were consummating, for example. And often times he broke into doubled-over laughter for no reason she could understand. When she asked him what was so funny he would say, "Sooner or later, lovely Molly. Sooner or later you'll know." Molly had no use for the cryptic. She would straighten him out on that account, first order of business. Scanning the room, then, with its sparse, cheap furnishings, she wondered how much money the Bastard actually had. According to him, anyway, it was quite a lot. But she would get to the bottom of that also; here was the second order of business.

The dressmaker was nearly through with her adjustment when she stuck Molly's ankle with a pin. Molly reeled and cursed her. A long silence, and neither woman moved.

"I'm sorry," said Molly finally. "I'm under a good deal of strain lately."

"I understand it perfectly," said the dressmaker. "Let's forget it ever happened."

But the dressmaker would not forget, and as she took up the hem she thought, *The slut screws her way into a fortune no one's even seen, and already she's putting on airs?* She decided to pad the bill, which made her feel somewhat but not completely better.

• • •

At this same moment, the Bastard stood in the center of the empty town, panting. He had broken into every storefront on the main street and stolen all he might carry with him. Several of the businesses kept safes, which he hadn't the time nor skill to open, and he was frustrated about this, but his satchel was filled with bills and coins and the most dazzling and exquisite jewelry, so he was not *too* terribly frustrated. He alley-ooped the heavy bag onto the back of Wilson's horse and tied this to the saddle. He mounted the horse and walked her in a tight circle. Looking out at the town, at the shards of plate glass glittering along the length of the road, he breathed in as deep as he might, then raised his head skyward and said loudly the very rudest word he knew. *Who in the world can know why this is, but God in heaven, it feels so good to say it,* he thought. Wilson's horse was all muscle as she ran. The Bastard ripped the tie from his neck and tossed it to the wind. Looking back, under his arm, he watched the ribbon of black silk spinning and dropping into the dusty wake, and this gave him satisfaction.

CONTRI

MARGARET JULL COSTA is a translator of Spanish and Portuguese literature, including the works of Javier Marías, José Saramago, Eça de Queiros, and Fernando Pessoa. In 2008, Costa won the PEN Translation Prize as well as the Weidenfeld Prize, thus netting the most important translation award on each side of the Atlantic in a single year.

PATRICK DEWITT's debut novel, *Ablutions*, is now available in paperback. His second novel, *The Sisters Brothers*, will be published by Ecco in 2011.

AARON JOHNSON is a painter based in Brooklyn. His reverse-painted acrylic-polymer-peel paintings inhabit the realms between the erotic-catastrophic/ecstatic-psychotic/comic-tragic, fusing diverse painting vocabularies into his own distinctive breed of Americana-grotesque, all rendered obsessively with tender brutality. Roberta Smith in The New York Times describes his works as "visceral, beautiful and flamboyantly timely, which is saying a lot." He is represented by Stux Gallery, New York; Irvine Contemporary, Washington DC; and Galleri Brandstrup, Oslo, Norway. Visit the artist's website: aaronjohnsonart.com

BILLY MALONE was born in Johnson City, Tennessee in 1968. He lives and works in New York City. His ballpoint pen drawings are included in the collections of the Whitney Museum of American Art, the Brooklyn Museum, and the Progressive Collection.

BUTORS

Admired by Bolaño, Ashbery, Sebald, and Coetzee, **JAVIER MARÍAS**, born in Madrid in 1951, is widely considered Spain's greatest living writer. He has been translated into thirty-seven languages and acclaimed here as "a rare gift" (*The New York Times Book Review*), "superb" (*Review of Contemporary Fiction),* "fantastically original" (*Talk*), "brilliant" (*Virginia Quarterly Review*), and "a true genius of literary subterfuge" (*The Village Voice*). New Directions has published nine of his books; forthcoming are the story collection, *While the Women Are Sleeping*, and the novella *Bad Nature, or, With Elvis in Mexico.*

ROBERTO RANSOM was born in Mexico City in 1960. He completed his undergraduate studies at the UNAM, School of Philosophy and Literature, and at La Salle's School of Religious Studies. He obtained his doctoral degree as a Fulbright-García Robles scholar at the University of Virginia. He presently holds tenure at the Autonomous University of Chihuahua, and teaches both in the Institute of Fine Arts and in the School of Humanities postgraduate program. He is a member of the Sistema Nacional de Creadores (Mexico's equivalent of the NEA). He has received an honorary mention from the National Institute of Fine Arts for his novel *En esa otra Tierra* (Alianza, 1991), and the National Prize for Children's Literature from the same institute in 2003, for *Joao y el Oso Antártica* (Alfaguara, 2006). He received the Chihuahua Prize for Literature for his short novel, *Los Días sin Bárbara* (Solar, 2006). Jasper Reid translated his novel/capricho *A Tale of Two Lions* and it was published by W. W. Norton in 2007 (El Aduanero, 1994). Dan Shapiro obtained an NEA Translator's Grant (2009) for the translation of Ransom's book of stories, *Missing Persons, Animals, and Artists* (*Desaparecidos, Animals, y Artistas*, El Guardagujas, CONACULTA, 1999). He is presently working on a book-length essay. He lives in Chihuahua with his wife and three children.

CONTRIBUTORS

DANIEL SHAPIRO is the translator of Roberto Ransom's *Desaparecidos, Animales, y Artistas (Missing Persons, Animals, and Artists).* Shapiro received translation fellowships from the NEA and PEN for Ransom's short story collection. His translations and poems have been published in *American Poetry Review* (Tomás Harris, cover feature, Sept/Oct 1997), *Black Warrior Review, BOMB, Confrontation, Poetry Northwest,* and *Yellow Silk*, as well as in *The Oxford Book of Latin American Poetry.* His translation of *Cipango*, by Chilean poet Tomás Harris, was published by Bucknell University Press in 2010. Shapiro is Director of the Department of Literature at the Americas Society in New York City and Editor of *Review: Literature and Arts of the Americas.*

BEN STROUD's stories have appeared or are forthcoming in *One Story, The American Scholar, Subtropics, Fiction, The Boston Review*, and other magazines. He has received residencies from Yaddo and the MacDowell Colony, and recently had a story selected for *New Stories from the South: The Year's Best, 2010.* A graduate of the University of Michigan's MFA program, he currently lives in Wiesbaden, Germany.

JOY WILLIAMS is the author of four novels, including *The Quick and the Dead*, which was a finalist for the Pulitzer Prize; three short story collections; and a book of essays, *Ill Nature.* She is a member of the American Academy of Arts and Letters.

SUB-●●
SCRIBE
●●●●TO
ELEC-●
●●TRIC
LIT-●●●
ERA-●●
●TURE!

Electric Literature is an anthology series of contemporary fiction. We select stories with a strong voice that capture our readers and lead them somewhere exciting, unexpected, and meaningful. And we publish everywhere, every way: paperback, Kindle, iPad/iPhone, and eBook.

Please use the form below to subscribe by mail, or go to electricliterature.com and subscribe online.

1) What's your name?

2) What issue would you like to begin your subscription with?

❒ Issue 1
Michael Cunningham, Jim Shepard, T Cooper, Diana Wagman, Lydia Millet

❒ Issue 2
Colson Whitehead, Lydia Davis, Marisa Silver, Stephen O'Connor, Pasha Malla

❒ Issue 3
Rick Moody, Aimee Bender, Patrick deWitt, Jenny Offill, Matt Sumell

❒ Issue 4
Joy Williams, Javier Marías, Roberto Ransom, Ben Stroud, Patrick deWitt

3) How would you like to receive Electric Literature?

PAPERBACK

❒ Within the USA and CANADA ($32) ❒ International ($64)

shipping address:

email address:

ELECTRONIC ($16)

choose a format: ❒ PDF ❒ ePub ❒ LRF ❒ Mobi

email address:

A subscription to Electric Literature is 6 issues.
Please make all checks payable to Electric Literature LLC

Send this form, or just write the information down on a piece of paper, and send it with a check to:

Electric Literature Subscriptions, 325 Gold St, Suite 303, Brooklyn, NY 11201

Ranked 15th in the country in 2009 by Poets & Writers, the M.F.A. program in Creative Writing at Brooklyn College has long been recognized for the caliber of our faculty and students. Our graduates publish widely, with their work recently represented in *The Best New Young Poets* anthology and *The Best American Short Stories*. Our playwrights have won Obies, started theater companies, and had their plays produced here and abroad.

The two-year program is small and select, with an emphasis on faculty mentoring. In addition to formal course work, students have the opportunity to work on the highly regarded *Brooklyn Review* and in internships. We offer cross-disciplinary readings by visiting writers and give our own students the opportunity to read and perform their works.

The program offers a number of fellowships as well as prizes and a winter writing residency at the Espy Foundation in Oysterville, Washington. Students in the program may also teach undergraduate courses for the English Department.

For further information, please visit our website at:
http://depthome.brooklyn.cuny.edu/english/graduate/mfa/geninfo.htm

CURRENT AND CONTINING FACULTY

FICTION:

Joshua Henkin, coordinator
Myla Goldberg
Colin Harrison
Amy Hempel
Fiona Maazel
Ernesto Mestre
Martha Nadell
Meera Nair
Jenny Offill
Nathaniel Rich
Ellen Tremper
Michael Cunningham
(program associate)

PLAYWRITING:

Mac Wellman, coordinator
Erin Courtney

POETRY WRITING:

Julie Agoos, coordinator
Ben Lerner
Marjorie Welish
Anselm Berrigan
Lisa Jarnot

Breinigsville, PA USA
21 June 2010
240314BV00002B/2/P

9 780982 498064